HEARTS AND SHADOWS

HEARTS AND SHADOWS

TARA GRAYCE

LCCN: 2026904226

ISBN: 978-1-943442-72-0

CHAPTER ONE

Princess Adeline of Kelverny curled on her divan in her sitting room. A book lay forgotten on her lap as she stared out the window looking east to the Pernell Mountains. From this distance, they looked so peaceful, a line of blue-purple crags outlined in ethereal white. She couldn't see the armies gathered on either side of the pass.

At a knock on her door, she closed the book and bade the person enter.

Thaddeus Wilks stepped into the room. A thatch of gray hair tufted above his slim face while a gathering of wrinkles framed his mouth. He was the only person in this entire castle she dared trust implicitly besides her personal maid. Before he'd been her personal secretary, he'd been her father's, before her father and mother had been killed in the Andur Pass five years before on a diplomatic mission to Lalsacia.

"Any word from Grandfather?" Adeline swiveled in

her seat to plant her feet on the floor in proper princess fashion. She chewed on her cheek as she waited for Thaddeus to answer. Her grandfather worried her. Even before her parents' deaths, he'd hated Lalsacia. In the wake of their deaths, he'd gone to war, ostensibly to avenge the death of his son and daughter-in-law. But everyone knew he was actually trying to claim the Donnaris Forest with its tiny fleech dragons.

Now his hatred burned with an intense fury. No peace would ever be satisfactory to him. He wanted to destroy the entire kingdom. He'd likely destroy the very woods and fleech dragons he'd started the war to gain.

Would he destroy Kelverny along the way?

Thaddeus folded his tall, bony frame onto one of the chairs across from her. "Still inspecting the army. He plans to be gone another week."

She nodded and stared back out the window. A gurgle of guilt swirled in her stomach. Only two weeks ago, Lalsacia had sent a party under a white flag of truce to discuss ending the hostility. Instead of a discussion, her grandfather had them arrested and thrown into the dungeon as spies. Before he'd left for the border, he had given the order for the guards to torture them to gain information about Lalsacia.

All of that was a gross violation of the accepted rules of war. Lalsacia wouldn't extend a hand of peace again after this. They, too, would be out for blood and destruction.

"I'm just so helpless, Thaddeus." Adeline resisted

the urge to push to her feet. Instead, she remained where she was, her legs daintily crossed at the ankles, even with only Thaddeus in the room. "I'm the crown princess of Kelverny, but I have no power."

Even her father, as much as he'd tried, hadn't been able to sway her grandfather when he set his mind to something. What could she do when no one but Thaddeus and Jelsa, her lady's maid, listened to her orders? When the crown landed on her head in the far distant future, would she truly be allowed to wield its authority? Or would the lords overrule her and force her to do their bidding?

There was a contingent of lords who were loyal to her father and thus to her, but they couldn't support her more until she was queen. While her grandfather lived, they were as helpless as she was.

Thaddeus leaned forward and patted her knee. "I know. Your day will come. Someday you'll stop this. I feel it."

She didn't feel so sure. What good was a crown if she became nothing but a pretty figurehead?

LORNE, PRINCE OF LALSACIA, SLOUCHED ON THE DUNGEON floor and flexed the fingers chained above his head. His back, chest, and ribs ached from the beatings he'd suffered since he'd been brought here. The cool stones of the wall behind him provided some relief, even as they chilled him.

The darkness closed around him, suffocating, all-consuming. The walls on either side were so close he could nearly brush them with his shoulders. When he stretched out his legs, his feet touched the solid wood door of his cell.

He'd been so foolish. His father had been right. The king of Kelverny wasn't ready to talk peace.

Guilt stabbed his chest along with the pain. His stubbornness had cost two good men their lives. They'd fought to protect him, but the Kelvernese sylon fighting cats had taken them down, ripping them apart before Lorne had been forced to surrender.

His foolishness in trying to bring about peace could cost still more lives. Would the Kelvernese kill his remaining guards one by one? And what would his father do to rescue his only son and heir?

Thankfully the Kelvernese didn't realize who they had. Not yet anyway.

They could never find out. If they did, they'd bring his father to his knees...and Lalsacia with him. Lorne's mission would end the war, but it would destroy Lalsacia in the process. The precious fleech dragons would be taken from their home in the Donnaris Forest and forced to do who knew what in the hands of the greedy king of Kelverny.

Lorne trusted his men not to talk. They were all battle-hardened warriors. They'd faced pain before, and they would hold up under whatever torture the Kelvernese king put them through.

No, Lorne was the weak link. He was the one who had to learn to be strong.

"Sir?" The voice filtered, faint, through the stones and thick wooden door of his cell.

Lorne swallowed, ran his tongue over his teeth, and tried to find enough breath to raise his voice. "Still here."

"Stay strong, sir."

Lorne couldn't bring himself to reply. His men had been doing that throughout this imprisonment, shouting encouragement to him, even though they were suffering just as much as he was.

They wouldn't say his name or call him *Highness*. But he had been dressed as a lord, clearly not one of the guards, so calling him *sir* and treating him as their leader wouldn't give away anything their Kelvernese torturers didn't already know.

They had to assume someone was listening at all times. There likely was a guard out in the passageway at this very moment.

The door of his cell rattled. He drew in as deep a breath as he could manage, gathering his courage to face more torture. *Stay strong.* His only choice was to stay strong or put his entire kingdom at jeopardy.

A slim old man, who looked too frail to hurt anyone, stepped into the cell. Not the usual brawny guards sent to whip and beat the words out of him. Lorne eyed the man. What torture did the Kelvernese have planned now?

The man drew out a waterskin, uncorked it, and poured a stream of liquid into a pewter cup. He knelt by Lorne. "You must be thirsty."

Lorne turned his face away. "I won't drink your poison."

The man's huff sounded like a laugh. He sipped from the cup. "It's just water. Not poison."

Lorne clenched his fists. What game was this? A ploy of kindness to weaken his defenses? His throat ached with thirst that urged him to take the offered water.

It shouldn't hurt to accept the water. He could play along, for now. He turned his face toward the man and allowed him to hold the cup to his mouth. He drained the cup in a few swallows, the water cooling the heat of his thirst.

The man rocked back on his spindly legs and studied him. "You want peace between Lalsacia and Kelverny?"

Lorne wasn't sure if he dared answer. But it wasn't a secret. He'd been on that mission riding into the Kelverny lines under a flag of truce. "Yes."

The man speared him with another look. "What would you be willing to do to achieve peace?"

Lorne raised his eyebrows. "So that's your game. Wheedle information out of me in the name of peace."

The man glanced toward the door then leaned closer. "Believe me. I have no love for this war. So I ask you. What would you be willing to do for peace?"

Lorne clamped his mouth shut, but he doubted it did any good. The man could read his answer in his eyes. He'd do just about anything to end this war.

The old man gave a nod before he poured more

water from the waterskin into the tin cup. He pressed it to Lorne's mouth again.

He was weak. So very weak. This time, he gulped the water down without hesitation.

Adeline dismissed her maid and brushed her own hair. The dark brown waves cascaded around her shoulders and down to her waist. If she closed her eyes, she could still remember the way her mother used to brush her hair when she was a child. Her mother's hair had been the same color, a memory of her that Adeline carried with her always.

Setting down her brush, she wrapped her arms around her waist, holding a knitted shawl over her shoulders, and walked from the dressing room, across her bedroom, and to her balcony, the doors standing open to let in the early summer night air.

A breeze whipped down from the distant mountains, cooling her skin. Somewhere, far away, the two armies were camped in that pass, resting from a day of battle and yet preparing to go back to fighting again the next day.

A commotion rose from the main gate, accompanied by the clack of horse hooves. The creak of the gates rang into the night a minute before a soldier cantered his horse into the courtyard, the mail of his armor gleaming beneath his coat of arms.

That was one of her grandfather's knights, but it

was too early for her grandfather to have returned. And this knight appeared to be alone.

Stepping away from the balcony's railing, she began to braid her hair. She hadn't changed into her nightgown yet, thankfully, so she only had to braid her hair to be somewhat presentable in case she was summoned.

Her fingers busy with her hair, she nudged open the door from her bedchamber to the sitting room with her shoulder before shutting it behind her with her slippered foot.

Almost as soon as she'd tied off the end of her braid, Thaddeus burst into her sitting room with barely a knock of warning.

She jumped and dropped the end of her braid. Her stomach twisted at the grim lines written across his face. "What's wrong?"

Thaddeus walked across the room and gripped her shoulders. "Lalsacia attacked while your grandfather was inspecting the army. He was badly wounded, and he isn't expected to make it."

The words sank in with the slow speed of dripping honey. She didn't feel any grief, not really. She knew she should. He was family. But she couldn't dredge up anything but the same regret that had plagued her relationship with her grandfather for years. "I should go to him."

"He isn't here yet. The wagon won't get here until the morning." Thaddeus hunched his shoulders.

A weight settled across her shoulders, even as she

slowly sat on her divan. She would be queen tomorrow. Kelverny would be hers to rule.

As that thought tingled though her, bile rose into her throat. "The law. We thought we'd have more time, but..." She swallowed. Kelverny had an ancient law of accession. Every king or queen had to be married to ascend to the throne. The law came from an old belief that marriage grounded a ruler in country and family.

With her grandfather healthy and seeming like he was going to rule for years, she'd thought she still had time to carefully weigh her marriage prospects. She'd been meeting the young men of the court, learning their alliances and politics, narrowing down those who would be an asset to the crown and those who would try to be the power behind it.

Now she had no time. Her grandfather had only hours, maybe days at most to live. With their country at war, she needed to ascend to the throne quickly.

She could see it now. The lords would descend on the castle in the morning. Each would be pressing his son or nephew on her. Or perhaps even himself, if he was under the age of eighty and unmarried. The council would band together and all but force her to marry their choice. She'd become little more than a puppet queen if they had their way.

If her grandfather lived more than a few hours, he would see to it that she married a man of his choice. A nobleman who would carry on the hatred of Lalsacia and continue the war.

She glanced into Thaddeus's eyes. "Who do you

think I should go with? Lord John Delaney or Lord Jasper Fellton?"

Through her careful deliberations and research, she had narrowed down her choices to those two men.

Lord John Delaney was a bit of a flake, but he wouldn't pressure her. He wouldn't be much of an asset, but he wouldn't try to rule her either. Still, she'd find herself rather alone in facing down the council, and he wouldn't be any help in ending the war or keeping her on the throne.

Lord Jasper Fellton was the son of one of the most powerful lords in the kingdom. If she married him, his father would back her...and strongarm her into doing things that would benefit him in return. If she was politically savvy, she could work with it. But it would be an exhausting way to live, and Lord Fellton the elder was a proponent of the war. He wouldn't push to end it.

Either way, she would likely find herself powerless. Or constantly locked in a power struggle with her own husband.

"What if there was a third option?" Thaddeus took the seat across from her, his gaze level as he held hers.

"Third option? Surely you don't mean Lord Lerroy?" Adeline resisted a shudder. Lord Lerroy wasn't a bad sort, all things considered. He was in his forties, fit, handsome, politically astute. Many a young woman married men old enough to be their fathers when politics demanded it.

But considering he was twenty years older than her, he would patronize her, never seeing her as a queen in her own right but instead as a child to be raised.

"No." Thaddeus drew in a deep breath. "Marry one of the Lalsacian peace party. Tonight."

"What?" Adeline nearly leapt to her feet before she sank back into the couch. "Surely you aren't serious."

"Quite serious." Thaddeus clasped his hands as he leaned his elbows on his knees. "The leader of the group is a Lalsacian lord. He's obviously trusted by his king."

"Yes, but..." Adeline's mind whirled as she tried to process everything. All her research, all her deliberations, she couldn't just throw it all away on a whim to marry some Lalsacian lord whom she knew nothing about. "The nobles wouldn't stand for it. They'd revolt before the year was out."

"Yes, they would." Thaddeus didn't even blink at that. "But nobles don't revolt the way peasants do. They plan a coup, and planning takes time. In that time, you can end the war. If you end the war, you not only consolidate your power, but you gain the undying loyalty of the commoners. The nobility wouldn't dare act against you then."

"You're asking me to risk everything—my kingdom, my life—for this?" Adeline's throat closed on the words. If she did as he suggested, it would be all or nothing. Either she succeeded or she plunged her kingdom not only into a continued war with its neighbor but also into a civil war. Not that she would live to see that civil war. She'd be dead long before it got to that point.

But if she succeeded? She could end the war. Build a lasting peace with Lalsacia. After all, she would've made one of their own the prince consort. Perhaps she could even convince Lalsacia to agree to have their crown prince marry a Kelvernese noblewoman.

Her parents had died trying to achieve a closer relationship with Lalsacia. They would have been appalled by how her grandfather had used their deaths as an excuse for war. How could Adeline do anything less than risk her own life to bring about peace?

She swallowed. It was a gamble. A gamble she'd have to live with for the rest of her life, no matter how long or short that life might be. She'd be tying herself to a man she didn't even know. If she survived, if she could bring about peace and retain her throne, then he would be her husband. He would have to be the father of her heir.

She squeezed her eyes shut. No matter what she did, she would have to marry a man she didn't love, whether it was this Lalsacian or someone else. She had no choice about that.

Her only choice was who and when. She could take the risk and marry the Lalsacian tonight, she could contact one of her other choices and marry him in the morning, or she could wait and let others decide her future for her.

She forced herself to meet Thaddeus's gaze. "Do you think the Lalsacian lord will go for it? We've treated him rather horribly."

By all rights, he would hate her after what her grandfather had done to him. Would he even want to help her bring about peace? Or would he just become one more danger she had to navigate? He might even kill her in her sleep and call it justified.

"Despite all he's been through, he's still committed to peace." Thaddeus gave a slight shake of his head, as if he couldn't quite believe it. "I talked to him briefly today."

"You talked to him? Why? We didn't know about Grandfather until a few minutes ago." Adeline searched Thaddeus's face.

For the first time, Thaddeus's gaze dropped. "I was investigating whether this could be an option, but I was expecting we'd have a few more days to consider it. You would've still had to marry him quickly, before your grandfather returned. But I never thought..."

Of course he hadn't. Who would've suspected she'd find herself with mere hours to make a decision like this?

"How do you know he's unmarried? If he's a well-respected lord in Lalsacia, then surely he's married with several children already." Adeline pictured someone like Lord Lerroy. A man in his forties. In his prime.

"I don't know for sure. It was something I was going to attempt to find out with further investigations." Thaddeus's grim look broke with a hint of a smile. "But he's young. Your age or maybe a handful of years older. Our odds are good that he isn't married yet, although he could be betrothed. It's hard to tell beneath the blood and grime, but he seems handsome."

Handsome was good. Not a great thing to base a marriage on, but right now, it was all she had.

There was no time for wavering. She had to take action now. This was her chance to take a step towards peace. No matter the cost to herself.

She straightened her spine and began winding her braid around her head. It wouldn't be as elegant as Jelsa's version, but a princess couldn't be seen wandering the castle with her hair down, even in a braid. "All right. I'll do it."

CHAPTER TWO

The muffled sounds of heavy footsteps in the passageway warned Lorne of the guards' approach, even before the lock to his cell rattled.

He squeezed his eyes shut, forcing his breathing to remain steady despite his racing heart. Not again. He wasn't ready. After that old man had left, the guards had come. And then...and then...

He couldn't hold up to much more. He simply couldn't. He was going to break, and he'd tell them everything. His kingdom would pay because he wasn't strong enough.

The door swung open, and light speared inside, so bright against the blackness that Lorne flinched even with his eyes already closed.

After a moment, Lorne cracked his eyelids open and squinted into the lamplight as one of the two guards wedged himself into the tiny cell, stepping around Lorne's legs, and reached for the chains pinning Lorne's hands above his head.

Lorne didn't resist as the guard unlocked his hands and immediately shackled them behind his back. The guard yanked him to his feet, and he had to mash his mouth shut to keep from whimpering at the pain shooting through his body.

He was dragged out of the cell, then hauled between the two guards down the now familiar corridor toward the just as familiar room at the end.

Another guard opened the door, and he staggered inside. The guards shoved him onto his knees so hard he couldn't help but give a cry of pain.

"That isn't necessary." A female voice—high-pitched and yet modulated—rang in the room, as out of place as a bouquet of flowers would have been.

Lorne managed to lift his head. A young woman stood near the center of the room, her back rigid, her dark brown hair wound in a braid around her head like a crown. The old man who had given Lorne water stood behind her.

The young woman made a gesture with her hand. "Please leave. I wish to speak with this man alone."

"Your Highness, he's—"

"Clearly not in any condition to be a danger to me." The young woman's voice rang with authority, her head high as she stared the guards down.

Lorne's skin prickled, his senses far more alert. There was only one person in Kelverny who held that title.

Crown Princess Adeline, the only heir of the current king of Kelverny.

Was this his chance? Would he finally get to talk to one of the members of the Kelvernese royal family?

The guards hesitated a moment longer before they left the room, closing the door after them.

Once the door was closed, Princess Adeline glanced around the room. Her mouth pressed into a tighter line as she picked up her skirt and took a step to the left, putting her farther away from the rather large bloodstain on the floor.

The sight shouldn't have sent a hard laugh welling in Lorne's throat. A sure sign all the torture and days in the dark dungeon were getting to him. But this princess was just so incongruous in her bright pink dress edged in white lace and stitched with gold thread in this place of blackness and torture.

That bloodstain was probably from him. And his men.

Remembering that quelled the chuckle before it became actual sound.

For a long moment, she stared at him, and he stared back. Should he make the first move? Or wait for her? Should he be defiant? Or conciliatory as he made a final bid for peace?

She drew in a deep breath, her shoulders straightening. "I am Crown Princess Adeline of Kelverny. I am sorry for what you and your men have endured."

"We came under a flag of truce." Lorne held her gaze, telling himself that he wasn't going to flinch away from a pair of deep brown eyes. Not after what he'd faced in the past weeks.

"I know." The stiff line of her shoulders remained, as did the upward tilt of her chin. "That was my grandfather's doing, not mine. I wish to bring about peace, not continue this war."

"A nice thought, but right now you don't even have the power to get me out of this dungeon." Lorne let the edge of bitterness coat his tone. Since being brought here, he'd learned more of the political situation, thanks to the chatter of the guards when they thought he was too out of it to hear.

Princess Adeline shared a look with the old man still standing behind her before she took a small step forward. "My grandfather has been mortally wounded while he was overseeing the army. Word is, he will be dead by morning. I will be queen tomorrow."

Then she would have power to halt the torture and actually listen to the diplomatic envoys this time. Assuming the lords didn't eat her alive the moment the crown landed on her head.

Did Lorne's father know that the Kelvernese king had been wounded? And how bad it was? Kelverny was about to be vulnerable as the crown transferred from the warmongering, strong king to this girl who, while poised and proper, didn't have the presence or power of her grandfather.

Lorne eyed her. There was something niggling at the back of his admittedly somewhat sluggish brain. "Isn't there some Kelvernese law about royal inheritance? Something about marriage..."

"Yes. To be crowned as queen, I must be married." Crown Princess Adeline remained serene and poised, even if something flashed through her eyes too quickly for Lorne to read. After a moment, her gaze sharpened more fully on him. "I would like to marry you. I believe true peace can only be achieved through such a drastic measure."

Oh. *Oh*. It took everything in him not to react. This princess had *no idea* what she was proposing. She didn't know that he wasn't a mere Lalsacian lord. He was its crown prince. Its only heir.

Since Crown Princess Adeline was Kelverny's only heir, their marriage would essentially unite their kingdoms. It wouldn't just be a mere peace. They would become one kingdom.

Was that what she wanted? Had Kelverny somehow discovered his real identity? It would be a brilliant move to marry him. She would gain the Donnaris Forest and the fleech dragons without ever launching a volley.

Yet he would also gain the sylon cats and the mines on the western side of the Pernell Mountains. He would someday be King of Lalsacia as she would be Queen of Kelverny. As long as their nobles didn't revolt over such a thing, they would co-rule the kingdoms together.

This could be peace. A lasting peace. He simply had to say yes and take the risk alongside her.

Besides, what other choice did he have? It was either marry her or break under torture, thus handing Kelverny the means to break his kingdom.

"Yes, I will marry you." He held her gaze without wavering. He'd do it. But he wasn't going to tell her who he was. Not yet. Not until he was sure he could trust her and this wasn't a ploy to gain his crown and kingdom.

Her shoulders slumped slightly as she released an exhale, the only sign of vulnerability before she drew herself straight once again. "Very well. Thaddeus will see to you. I'm afraid the wedding is somewhat clandestine."

Of course it was. She likely didn't yet have the power to truly release him from the dungeon against her grandfather's orders. Perhaps the guards would be bribed or she had a few on her side. Nor would most of her nobles stand for a midnight marriage to an enemy, even if no one but him would know the true political ramifications of this wedding.

"I understand." Lorne's knees ached from kneeling on the stone. But this would all be over soon.

Before morning, he'd be married to the enemy princess.

A NEW SET OF GUARDS ARRIVED SHORTLY AFTER THE PRINCESS and her steward left. These guards hauled him up the dungeon stairs and through what felt like every deserted corridor in the castle before he was shoved into a room, his shackles finally removed. He stumbled and collapsed to his knees, too weak to stay standing.

As he rubbed his bruised and reddened wrists, the

door behind him shut with the distinct click of the lock sliding into place. Good to know where he stood. He might be marrying the princess, but he wasn't trusted. Not by a long shot.

Then again, he didn't trust them either so at least they were well matched in that regard.

The room was opulent enough. He appeared to be in a sitting room, and he could see the opening to a bedchamber beyond. Several plush chairs and couches surrounded the thick rug where he knelt while tapestries featuring stylized sylon cats covered the walls.

Behind him, the lock clicked again a moment before the door opened. This time, Thaddeus stepped inside with a leather bag over a shoulder. A guard followed with a steaming kettle in one hand while another guard lingered by the door, prepared to step in if the enemy prince proved to be hostile.

Lorne kept one arm pressed to his stomach to somewhat contain the pain of his ribs. He would have laughed, but that would have hurt far too much. He wasn't in any shape to attack anyone. Right now, even Thaddeus could take him.

The guard set the kettle on a porcelain tile on a side table. He lingered for a moment until Thaddeus gave him a nod and gestured to the door. With one last glance, the guard left, closing the door after him.

"Come. Sit." Thaddeus pointed at the couch closest to the side table. "I'm afraid we don't have enough time to properly tend your wounds, but let's get you cleaned up enough to make it through the ceremony."

Lorne gathered himself enough to push to his feet. He took two steps and fell more than sat on the couch. He remained sitting upright rather than lying down. He didn't trust this man enough to be that vulnerable.

And, well, if he lay down, he wasn't sure he'd have the strength to get up again.

Thaddeus set his bag on the table before he bustled into the bedchamber, returning a moment later with a porcelain basin. He set it on the table before he poured steaming water from the kettle into it.

Grimacing, Lorne struggled to untie the laces of his shirt. He managed to twist enough to get one of his arms partially out of the sleeve, but then...he got stuck. Humiliatingly stuck with his shirt wrapped around him as if he were a child who couldn't undress himself.

Thaddeus reached out and helped him untangle himself. After some tugging—and a few cries of pain—Thaddeus finally drew a knife and cut the shirt off. Much of it was still stuck to the dried blood and open wounds on Lorne's back and across his chest.

With a shake of his head, Thaddeus returned to the table and dipped a rag in the water. "We'll worry about the rest of it after the ceremony when the physician can tend you. If we try to peel all that off now, we'll reopen your wounds and you'll likely bleed through the bandages during the ceremony. Here, clean up your face and hands as much as you can."

Lorne took the rag and scrubbed his face, his movements slow and pained. Even lifting his hand to his face ached in his stiff shoulders and sent stabs of agony through his ribs.

At least he could put off the pain of properly tending his wounds for a while longer. With the way the remnants of his shirt were embedded into the crusts of blood, that was going to hurt nearly as much as the actual torture had.

After Lorne had managed to clean up some of the blood and grime of the dungeon from his face and hands, Thaddeus helped him change into clean clothes and spritzed him with a hint of cologne to hide the unwashed, dungeon smell as much as possible.

And just like that, Lorne was as ready for his wedding as he could be.

CHAPTER THREE

Adeline tried to sit still as Jelsa tucked pearls into the braid still wound around her head. "This isn't necessary. You'll just have to take all these out in a few minutes."

"Yes, Your Highness. But you deserve to feel pretty at your wedding. Even one such as this." Jelsa continued positioning the pearls, setting them in such a way that the combination of braid and pearls formed a semblance of a crown. "It is too bad you can't wear a tiara."

By rights, Adeline was entitled to wear a tiara on her wedding day. But the royal tiaras were stored in the vault, and requesting one would mean going through her grandfather's steward and the vault guards. Neither of those things would be good for keeping this wedding a secret.

Instead, she'd have to make do with the personal jewelry items she had in her own room.

"It's all right, Jelsa." Adeline smoothed her hands

over the silk skirts of the pink dress she wore. It wasn't nearly as intricate as a royal wedding dress would have been, but it, too, would have to do. She didn't wish to take the time to change, and this particular dress was one of her favorites. "Thank you for being here tonight."

"Of course, milady. Anything for you." Jelsa adjusted a few strands of Adeline's hair before she reached for the cosmetics.

Adeline held still as Jelsa dusted her face with powder, but she thankfully didn't do more than that. Less to clean off in a handful of hours.

A knock sounded on the outer door a moment before it opened. Thaddeus's voice called from the other room, "Your Highness, everything is ready."

Adeline took one last look at herself in the mirror. The pearls glimmered in the lamplight where they were nestled against her dark brown hair while the powder emphasized the pallor of her porcelain complexion.

Everything might be ready, including her outward appearance. But inside, she was far from ready.

She had to be strong. This was what her kingdom needed. It was her best political move, despite the risk.

Pushing to her feet, Adeline smiled at Jelsa before she forced herself to totter on shaking legs from her dressing room, through her bedchamber, and into her sitting room.

Thaddeus stood before the door, and when his gaze landed on her, he dipped into a bow so low he should only have given it to his reigning sovereign. "My queen."

"Not yet." Adeline gestured for him to rise.

"But soon." Thaddeus straightened and held out an arm. "We must hurry."

Just the words that every girl wants to hear before her wedding.

Adeline took Thaddeus's arm, and he led her into the corridor. Bustle and noise came from the intersection of the corridors where the king's chambers lay. Likely his servants and guards preparing for his return. Many of the nobility would be descending soon, if they weren't already.

After a glance around, Adeline and Thaddeus headed farther down the passageway in the other direction before taking the servants' stairs down to the ground floor. There, they stuck to the back corridors until they stepped through a side door into the assembly hall. It wasn't as large as the newer Great Hall, but it was the original grand hall of the castle and the traditional place where the monarchs of Kelverny were married. It was also used as the place where the monarch met with the council.

In the rows before the dais stood a few of the guards, servants, and lords she trusted to be loyal to her.

Well, they were loyal to her late father and thus to her by default.

As she and Thaddeus strode down the center aisle, the guards and servants in the back rows bowed to her. She nodded to them, acknowledging their loyalty.

She halted by the front rows to greet the lords gathered there. There was only a handful of them, and sadly none of them had unmarried sons or grandsons over the age of eighteen, otherwise she would have married into one of their families in a heartbeat.

But those lords could be the difference between a coup and retaining her throne. Between death and actually surviving the next few years to bring peace.

Once the greetings were finished, she squared her shoulders and faced the dais. There, the only court official she trusted stood beside a young man she only vaguely recognized as the same man she'd met only an hour ago in the dungeon. He wore clean clothes, even if they were ill-fitting. She could only guess where Thaddeus had gotten them. The young man's hair was smoothed down, his face mostly clean. He was still somewhat bent over, one arm pressed over his ribs, as if he was struggling to remain standing.

Gripping her skirts, Adeline climbed the stairs and halted before her groom. Thaddeus remained at the base of the dais, stepping off to the side in the place of a servant rather than the father-figure he'd become in the past five years.

Adeline didn't reach for her groom's hands, nor did he offer them. The two of them simply stared at each other, two strangers only bound by their desire for peace between their kingdoms. And soon, bound together in marriage.

LORNE TOOK IN HIS BRIDE'S PALE CHEEKS, THE TREMBLING IN her fingers that she tried to hide by clasping her hands demurely before her. She was terrified, and yet she was here, going through with this.

The sight twisted something inside him. He was alone here, but so was she. This might be her kingdom, her castle, and her people, but she stood alone. No family besides the dying grandfather. No one loyal to her but the small gathering in this room. If they didn't succeed, she very well could find herself losing not just her throne but also her life.

Yet she was gambling on him. On an enemy.

He tried to straighten as much as he could as the court official began the ceremony. Perhaps realizing that Lorne wouldn't remain standing for long or maybe knowing their time was limited before someone sent for the princess, the officiant hurried through the formal ceremony, coming to the vows all too soon.

"Do you..." The officiant halted, staring at Lorne as if realizing for the first time that no one knew his name.

Lorne tried to calm his racing heart, to keep his face neutral, his voice level. "Lord Lorne of Chapend."

He held his breath, waiting. Would they recognize the name? How much of the royal family's name did the Kelvernese know?

His full name was Crown Prince Philip Alexander Lorne Chevalric of the Royal House of Dorrialle. But he always went by Lorne with his family and friends since his father's name was also Philip. The Chapend title was one of his lesser titles.

But if he wanted this marriage to be legal and binding once he revealed the truth, then he needed to use enough of his real name for it to hold up. He didn't want to risk his own gamble by giving her reason to annul the marriage the moment she learned the truth.

Neither the officiant nor the princess reacted to the name to give away any shock or recognition.

Instead, the officiant continued in the same tone, "Do you, Lord Lorne, take Princess Adeline Georgette Heraldron to be your wife?"

"I do." He tried to put as much strength into the words as he could.

The officiant turned slightly toward Princess Adeline. "And do you, Princess Adeline, take Lord Lorne of Chapend to be your husband?"

"I do." She lifted her chin, as if in defiance of something or someone. Of Lorne? Or perhaps her grandfather and all those who wished to continue this war?

With a few short words, the officiant wrapped up the ceremony and declared them married.

Thaddeus presented them with various paperwork they had to sign to make it official. Holding his breath, Lorne scrawled his real name, hoping his natural scribbling and the added shakiness from his weakness disguised the name enough that no one would realize just who he was.

No one scrutinized the paperwork that closely. Not even the various lords and witnesses that the court official called forward to also sign the paperwork to make it doubly official.

Almost as soon as they finished signing everything,

the court official added his seal, as did Princess Adeline. Then he rolled up the paperwork, saying something about making sure it got filed and registered properly that night. He hurried off, even as some of the lords stepped forward.

Lorne tried to smile, tried to straighten, as the lords greeted him, their gazes sizing him up. These lords were committed to their princess and the goal of peace, but they weren't yet convinced that this was the right course.

But the longer he stood there, the more black spots danced before his vision. Breathing was growing harder, his ribs stabbing more painfully, his legs growing shakier.

He didn't even realize he was collapsing until Thaddeus was there, the old man propping him up. He barely registered Princess Adeline dismissing the others as Thaddeus and one of the guards began hauling him, staggering, from the dais.

He'd survived his wedding. Now to see if he would survive the consequences.

ADELINE TRAILED AFTER THADDEUS, THE GUARD, AND HER new husband—Lord Lorne—through the back corridors to her room.

When they entered her sitting room, she hurried around the others, striding straight through her bedchamber and into the dressing room beyond. She sank onto the chair before the mirror, releasing a long exhale as she did. A shudder swept through, a shaking that started at her core and went outward into her hands, her knees, her legs, until she was hunched over her dressing table, gasping in quick breaths.

"Oh, milady." Jelsa hurried across the room to her. Her hands fluttered for a moment, as if she didn't know what to do.

Adeline squeezed her eyes shut. She wanted a mother who could hug her in this moment. She wanted a friend who wasn't a servant and could offer true comfort. She wanted a husband who wasn't a stranger and an enemy. She wanted a kingdom that wasn't in the midst of a war of their own making.

All foolish wishes. She was a crown princess, and a crown princess didn't have the luxury of wants and wishes. Just the weight of duty that would only grow heavier on the morrow once she became queen.

Still shuddering, Adeline tried to pull herself together. She couldn't fall apart like this. This night was far from over.

Straightening, she lifted her chin once again. As if understanding her wish for a moment of quiet, Jelsa silently picked all of the pearls from Adeline's hair. Once done, she unwound the braid, taking out the pins, so that it now lay down her back.

"Do you wish me to help you into a nightgown?" Jelsa didn't do something as obvious as glance at the door to the bedchamber, but something in her stance gave her thoughts away.

Tonight, there would be a man in Adeline's chamber. In her bed.

True, she had every expectation that that man was in no shape for pressing any advances.

If only she could have told Thaddeus to put Lord Lorne in the connecting room to her own. But there must be no doubt that this marriage was valid, starting with sharing her room with the lord for at least these first crucial days.

"No. Help me into a day dress." Hopefully one of those would be loose and comfortable enough for sleeping, should she find herself drifting off. "I will be called to my grandfather's side as soon as he arrives. I'd rather remain dressed for that."

"Yes, milady." Jelsa disappeared deeper into the room for a moment as she searched through the dresses, finally pulling out a day dress in a soft yellow.

Perfect. It was old and at the point where she didn't wear it often anymore. But it was exactly what she needed for tonight.

As Jelsa started helping Adeline out of her ruffled, pink evening gown, the outer door opened and shut, followed by the sound of male voices.

That was likely the physician. He wasn't the royal physician, as that man was waiting in her grandfather's chamber for him to arrive. Nor did she trust the royal physician enough to send for him for something clandestine.

Instead, this physician was the one who tended the guards and the servants. He was a brother to one of her personal guards, and both he and his brother were loyal enough to her for her to risk sending for him.

Once out of her evening gown, Adeline pulled the day dress over her head, tying the front laces loosely.

With that done, she took a deep breath and forced herself to walk on shaking legs to the door between her dressing room and bedchamber. Her hand trembling, she lifted the latch and tugged the door open just as a cry of pain rang out in the other room.

Her groom lay on his side on the bed, his back to where she stood. As he no longer wore a shirt, she got a good look at his broad shoulders...and the mess of red gashes and scabs that covered his back from his neck all the way to the waistline of his trousers.

The physician had pulled up a chair to the bed and was currently dabbing at Lord Lorne's abdomen with a rag, which came away bloody. Thaddeus stood beside him, holding a candle to provide more light.

At the sound of the door, or perhaps her gasp, both the physician and Thaddeus looked up.

"Highness." The physician bowed as much as he could while sitting down. Coming from him, it wasn't an oversight but a practicality. "Perhaps you should wait in the sitting room. This will not be...pleasant."

"I understand that." Adeline forced herself to walk closer, aiming for the bed rather than the door. "But he is my husband. I need to see what my grandfather did to him."

Lord Lorne and his men had crossed the border under a flag of truce. This never should have happened to him or the others.

Her grandfather would argue that her parents had been riding under a flag of truce when they'd been killed in an unprovoked attack when their kingdoms hadn't even been at war yet. But returning Lalsacian war crimes with war crimes of their own was no way to fight a war.

"Then if you are going to stay, I could use another set of hands, if you are willing to lend your maid." The physician turned his attention back to his work, pressing the rag to a wound.

Lord Lorne jolted, muffling his cry by pressing his face to the pillow.

Her stomach swooped into her toes, but she forced herself forward. "Jelsa may help if she wishes, but I would like to help as well."

No matter how much her stomach churned, she needed to do this. This man was now her husband. Perhaps that didn't mean much to him, but it did to her. She'd made her choice, and she desperately needed him to be her ally. And she couldn't expect him to be that if she wasn't that to him as well.

She carefully climbed onto the bed and crawled across the large mattress to sit next to Lord Lorne's back, trying not to jostle the bed, and thus him, too much.

This close, she could see all too well when the physician grasped what appeared to be a stained bit of cloth stuck to gaping wounds across Lorne's stomach and yanked.

Lord Lorne flinched and cried out again. Thaddeus leaned forward and grasped Lord Lorne's wrist before he could shove the physician away.

"Jelsa, could you please fetch me a basin and hot

water? I can begin washing his back." Adeline somehow kept her voice somewhat steady, despite the flipping in her stomach.

Standing in the doorway of the dressing room, Jelsa bobbed a curtsy before she hurried toward the door to the sitting room. "Yes, milady."

Lord Lorne turned his head, cracking one eye open to peer at her. "You don't have to stay."

"You don't have to guard my sensibilities. I can handle this." Adeline forced her voice to remain calm, collected.

Lord Lorne squeezed his eyes shut again as the physician swiped at the now bleeding gash. "It's my pride I was thinking of, more than your sensibilities."

"I think neither of us has the luxury of pride in our current situation." Adeline wasn't quite sure what to do with her hands until Jelsa returned with the basin and water. It seemed presumptuous to offer him comfort.

"Perhaps." He bit off the word before curling in on himself under the physician's administrations. "I certainly won't have much by way of dignity left."

Adeline wasn't sure how to respond to the joking, lighter note in his voice. She wouldn't have expected it, given their short acquaintance, the fact that they were enemies, and his present injured state.

She let the pause linger as the physician finished cleaning the gashes across Lord Lorne's stomach.

"What caused those?" She gestured toward the gashes, now seeping blood.

"Sylon cat." Lord Lorne's voice was slightly slurred,

his eyes closed once again. Some of the tension had faded from his face, his muscles more relaxed than they'd been moments ago. "They set sylon cats on us to capture us. One attacked as I was surrendering."

"And your back?" Adeline wasn't sure she wanted to know. And yet she would be queen within days, if not hours. She couldn't shy away from seeing the horrors of things like this.

"Whipped." The word was so slurred it was barely understandable. "Also beaten."

"Is something wrong?" Adeline glanced from Lord Lorne, who seemed to be slipping away, to the physician.

"Not to worry. I gave him a tincture to help with the pain. It's working." The physician prodded at Lord Lorne's ribs, which earned a low moan and a flinch, though the moan wasn't nearly as loud as the cries from earlier.

"The stuff feels nice," Lord Lorne murmured. "Not as nice as a fleech dragon. I can see why you'd kill for them. But they're precious. Can't be...be..."

He seemed to have lost his train of thought, his breathing slowing and steadying.

According to the legends she'd heard, fleech dragons had a magic that eased pain, sent a peaceful calm through a person, and perhaps even healed, if the stories coming out of Lalsacia were true. She'd never experienced it herself, of course. But it was one of the reasons fleech dragons were so highly prized and worth starting a war for, at least to people of her grandfather's ilk.

There was something tragically ironic about starting a war over dragons who gave peace and healing with their magic.

"How bad off is he?" Adeline took in the gashes, the bruises, the network of torn skin across his back. Had she married a lord who was promptly going to die on her?

As long as he lived long enough for the crown to land on her head, she'd fulfill the law. She wasn't required to remarry to remain queen, although she would eventually need an heir.

Yet that wouldn't help her forge peace with Lalsacia. It might even hurt her chances, if the Lalsacian emissary promptly died after she married him, even if his death wasn't her doing.

"While he isn't in mortal danger, I am concerned." The physician pointed to the gashes. "These are enflamed and should have been cleaned long before now. Same for his back. Several of his ribs are broken, and I can only guess how much bruising and damage he sustained to his internal organs. He will need a great deal of rest, and we can only hope the infection hasn't set in too deeply."

The door opened, and Jelsa returned with the requested hot water and basin. She balanced the items on the bed next to Adeline and handed her a rag.

Adeline dabbed at the blood on Lord Lorne's back. After a few minutes, Jelsa nudged her aside and took over, scrubbing far harder and more thoroughly than Adeline would have.

She didn't know how long it took to clean all the

wounds and bind them with salve and bandages. By the time the physician finished and left with Thaddeus, Adeline blearily cleaned her own hands in the fresh water Jelsa brought, dismissed her maid, and collapsed onto the other side of the bed, too tired to even care that there was a man sleeping nearby.

CHAPTER FOUR

"Highness. Your Highness."

Someone was shaking her, gently at first, then more firmly. Adeline groaned and blinked into the fuzzy brightness of a candle held far too close to her face. "What is it?"

"Your grandfather has arrived, milady." Jelsa released Adeline's shoulder and stepped back. "You will wish to hurry. He will send someone to fetch you at any moment."

The words jolted Adeline awake so thoroughly that she found herself on her feet before she'd fully registered what she was doing.

She could not have one of the lords invade her room in the name of bringing her to the king. Right now, it would be best if no one knew she had a Lalsacian lord in her bed. At the moment, the fact that he wasn't in the dungeon was somewhat treasonous as she was going against the king's orders. It would be fine once she was queen and could undo those orders, but until her grandfather died, she'd be in a precarious position.

She glanced over her shoulder at where Lord Lorne lay still on the bed, his face pale despite his darker skin tone. The only sign that he was still alive was the steady rise and fall of his chest beneath the blanket.

Jelsa hurriedly tucked a few strands of Adeline's hair back into her braid. "I wish I could do more, Highness."

"It is just as well. It would look suspicious if I was too highly made up at this time of morning, even with the warning of the messenger." Adeline pulled herself straighter, gathering herself as she forced her mind to function. "But perhaps a shawl?"

"Yes, milady." Jelsa disappeared into the dressing room, returning a moment later with a long, gray shawl. A properly somber color without yet going into full mourning. While the yellow day dress was hardly somber, it was at least a nod to the Kelvernese royal color of deep yellow.

"Thank you." Adeline wrapped the shawl around her shoulders just as a knock sounded on the outer door of her suite.

Jelsa hurried from the room and across the sitting room, and Adeline followed at a slower pace. She closed the door to her bedchamber after her, standing off to the side.

Cracking the door open, Jelsa dipped her head respectfully. "Yes, milord?"

"The princess has been summoned to attend her

grandfather." Lord Sarlon's whining, supercilious tone grated over Adeline's skin.

She lifted her chin high and swept to the door, not flinching when Lord Sarlon gave her an assessing look from head to toe, the pinch in his brows saying that he found her wanting.

He spun on his heel and set off down the corridor, and Adeline followed. Likely she should be the one leading him as she outranked him, but she was too tired to engage in that battle just yet.

Appearing out of the darkness farther down the corridor, Thaddeus gave her a nod before he slipped into her room. At least Lord Lorne wouldn't be left fully alone.

Jelsa and one of her guards trailed after her, and something eased inside her at the fact that she wouldn't be alone with the lord. Or with her grandfather.

The corridor ended in a large space where several of the main corridors connected. The doors for the king's palatial apartments and the consort's suite opened from this foyer.

The door to her grandfather's chambers stood open as a revolving hustle of scribes, secretaries, stewards, guards, court officials, and lords scurried in and out. The bustle halted as she glided through the doorway, everyone pausing what they were doing to bow or curtsy to her.

She didn't stop to acknowledge them, not even with a nod. Her focus remained on the door across the expansive sitting room. That door, too, hung open, and the royal doctor stood beside the bed, a bloody bandage in his hand.

After all the blood and injuries she'd seen the night before, she shouldn't quail before this. Yet her hands still trembled where she had them clasped before her, and her stomach still flipped as she stepped into the bedchamber and smelled the musty odor of blood and the sour stench of a festering wound.

Her grandfather lay on his bed, the covers only drawn to his waist. A deep gaping wound slashed across his stomach, and Adeline had to look away before she caught more than a glimpse. This wound wasn't at all like those Lord Lorne had suffered. His had scored through skin and muscle, but this one showed internal things that should never see the light of day.

She brought her gaze up to her grandfather's face. He seemed so wan and drawn, so unlike the powerful force of a man that he usually was.

Yet when he turned his head and focused on her, his brown eyes still burned with the intensity that never failed to make her retreat within herself. "Adeline. Come here, girl."

She tiptoed closer to the bed, avoiding the doctor as he continued his gruesome work. "Yes, Grandfather?"

"I am dying, or so the doctor tells me." Her grandfather sent a scathing look at the royal doctor, as if he blamed him for not being able to save him from such ghastly wounds.

The doctor gave a slight shake of his head as he laid out fresh bandages.

Adeline managed a nod for her grandfather. He wasn't looking for more of a response than that anyway.

"It's time to stop avoiding the question of your marriage." Her grandfather gave a grimace, though not all of his expression seemed directed at her.

Still, the sign of pain was far less than she would have expected, given how much pain Lord Lorne had been in from his more minor injuries.

But perhaps the lack of pain was a bad sign, the injury so deep he no longer felt it. Or maybe the doctor had dosed him so strongly he was all but numb.

"For that reason, I have betrothed you to Lord Sarlon's second son." Grandfather made a weak motion with his hand.

For the first time, she noticed that Lord Sarlon had followed her into the room, but he had remained near the foot of the bed. Now he stepped forward, his hands clasped behind his back. "Jonas is greatly honored by this betrothal."

Adeline swallowed. Jonas, Lord Sarlon's second son, was a spoiled, blustering bully of a young man who did whatever his father and her grandfather told him to do. He was the last man in court she wanted to marry, knowing that Jonas would do his best to ensure she did whatever his father wanted. She'd be Lord Sarlon's puppet queen.

Her grandfather knew that, but he also knew that Lord Sarlon would continue the war and force her rule to follow in his footsteps. This was her grandfather's way of exerting control over her, even after his death.

Adeline forced her shoulders to remain straight, her chin high. She'd already undercut her grandfather's plans by marrying the Lalsacian lord. This betrothal was invalid since she was already married.

But now wasn't the time to announce that yet. Her grandfather was still far too alert and too in power. He could still solve the problem by ordering Lord Lorne's execution.

Adeline dipped her chin in the slightest of nods. "As I am of age, Grandfather, you will need my consent and my signature on this betrothal. If I may have a copy of the paperwork, I would like time to consider this."

"If you must." Grandfather used that dismissive tone, the one that suggested she should feel guilty for daring to assert herself that much. "But make your decision soon. I will see you married before I die."

One of her grandfather's secretaries stepped forward and placed a stack of papers in her hands. It was rather thick for a betrothal contract, and she wondered just what her grandfather had negotiated away on her behalf.

"If that is all, I would like to take my leave." Adeline clutched the papers and waited. Her grandfather had long ago lost the privilege of having her wait by his deathbed. But he was still king and held all the power. She couldn't leave until he dismissed her. "I have these to peruse."

"Very well. Go. That contract is above your comprehension anyway. I suppose you will need the time to have someone explain it to you." Her grandfather made that motion with his hand again, brushing her off as brusquely as he always did, even if the underlying weakness betrayed him in the way he dropped his shaking hand back to the blanket.

Adeline turned and met the doctor's gaze. "Summon me if there's any change."

The doctor nodded. "I will, milady."

With that, Adeline walked from the room as quickly as she dared, Jelsa and the guard trailing after her once again. In the corridor, she quickened her pace until she was finally stepping into the safety of her own rooms.

Once the guard closed the door behind her, she released a long exhale, her posture slumping.

Thaddeus hopped to his feet from where he'd been sitting in one of the chairs. "Are you all right, milady? I heard your grandfather has arrived."

"He has." Adeline strode farther into the room. "How is..." She trailed off and gestured to the bedchamber door, strangely unwilling to say his name or anything about him out loud, not after just coming from her grandfather's side.

"Still sleeping." Thaddeus's gaze searched her face, probably reading how wounded she felt after even those few minutes with her grandfather, even if the interaction had been blessedly short. Her grandfather had been too injured to take the time to berate her over her hair or her dress, even if he'd still belittled her intelligence. "I have called the physician to attend him when he has a moment. And when he thinks he can sneak in."

"Thank you." Adeline sank onto the chair across from him, waiting while he retook his seat. Then she held up the thick mass of papers. "My grandfather has betrothed me to Lord Sarlon's son. It isn't official until I sign it, which I won't, of course. But I told them I needed to read it over and contemplate my decision. Based on how thick this is, my grandfather must have granted Lord Sarlon more than a few concessions. We'll need to read this over, ensure there is nothing in here that will legally hurt me when I end it, and see what he wants so that I can negotiate a different appeasement to hold Lord Sarlon off until I can solidify my power."

Thaddeus nodded and held out a hand. "Let's get started, then."

Adeline handed him the second half of the stack. He might be a little lost, picking up halfway through without the earlier context, but he'd figure it out.

THE PAIN YANKED HIM FROM SLEEP. LORNE CLAMPED HIS teeth around his moan as he blinked his eyes open.

"Hold still. I'm almost finished." A deep male voice reverberated above him, and it took him far longer than it should have to recognize the physician from the night before.

Was it only the night before? Lorne's mouth felt strangely dry and gummy, his body cold and achy, despite the soft mattress beneath him and blanket over him.

He bit back another moan as the physician spread salve over his wounds.

"I'm sorry. I will give you more of the tincture in a few minutes." The physician kept at his work without a pause. "But the princess wished to speak with you once you woke."

The Kelvernese princess. Lorne's wife. Just what had he done last night?

As the physician wrapped bandages around Lorne's torso, the bedchamber door cracked open, and Adeline's voice filtered inside. "How is he?"

"Awake, if you wish to speak with him." The physician lifted Lorne's shoulders slightly to wrap the bandage around him.

Lorne tried to prop himself onto an elbow to help, but all of his muscles felt shaky and weak. Was it his imagination that he felt worse than before?

The door opened all the way, and Adeline glided inside, dressed in a somber gray gown that was edged in black lace. Her grandfather must have arrived during the night. Was the man still alive or had he already passed?

Her gaze landed on him. "How are you feeling?"

He might have been more embarrassed about his undressed state, especially since he currently lay in her bed, if he hadn't felt so terrible. He attempted a smile. "Not great."

"He's developed a fever that has me concerned." The physician tied off the bandage and lowered Lorne back onto the pillow. "We will need to ensure he is given plenty of liquids and has lots of rest."

A fever. That would explain the shivering taking hold of him. He shook, even as the physician placed the blanket over him once again.

If only he had a fleech dragon. Then he'd be fine.

Instead, he might still die, even now. He supposed that as long as he outlived the Kelvernese king, his death wouldn't matter to Adeline.

But it would be catastrophic for Lalsacia. His father would be robbed of his only heir, and he wouldn't even know until Kelverny returned Lorne's body. If they ever did.

Adeline crept closer to the bed before she perched at the very edge near his feet. "Please do whatever you can for him."

She looked small, curling in on herself even if her back remained straight, her chin lifted. He would have reached for her hand if they'd had that kind of relationship. And if she'd sat close enough for such a gesture.

"I will, Highness." The physician paused in packing up his items to give her a bow. "I will step out for a moment to prepare the tincture. I would also like to get some willow bark tea into him."

"Send Jelsa to fetch it. I wouldn't trust anyone else right now." Adeline motioned toward the other room.

The physician nodded again before he left, closing the door softly behind him.

Adeline's gaze dropped to her lap, her fingers twisting there as she remained silent.

Lorne gathered his strength enough to force a few more words from his dry mouth. "He called you *Highness*."

"I'm not yet queen, I'm afraid." She didn't look at him, but the hunched look to her grew more pronounced. "My grandfather has arrived. He seems to be lingering on sheer spite and anger, but the doctor isn't optimistic. I will be queen before tomorrow morning, if not before the day is out."

Even once her grandfather was dead, her war would only be just beginning. She would be in a fight for her life, her crown, and the peace she hoped to achieve.

Last night, he'd pledged to do whatever he could do to help her in that war. There wasn't much he could do at the moment, but perhaps simply offering her a moment of comfort was enough. After all, everyone else around her was either a loyal subject or a potential enemy. Except for him. He was her equal. Her husband.

He freed his right hand from the blankets, shivering as the cold air prickled against his skin. He held his hand out to her, palm up. "You aren't alone. I am your ally, even if that doesn't count for much right now."

Adeline's gaze finally lifted, her brown eyes meeting his, both searching and vulnerable. She didn't take his hand, but something in her softened. "Thank you."

He managed a hint of a nod before he twitched his hand toward where the pitcher and a glass sat on a sideboard. "Could I have some water?"

"Oh, of course." Adeline hopped to her feet and scurried to the sideboard. She poured some of the water into a glass and turned, pausing. Her already pale cheeks first went even paler before staining pink. She glided back across the room, hesitated a moment, and perched on the bed next to him this time, close enough that he could feel the warmth of her against his arm.

Lorne tried to prop himself onto an elbow, but his arm shook, his whole body quaking with a stronger shiver.

She slid her hand behind his head, her fingers warm as they threaded through his hair. But the glass was cold, the water even colder as it sloshed into his mouth.

He gulped at the water, some of it dribbling out of the sides of his mouth. But he was too thirsty to care about dignity at the moment.

When he coughed and sputtered, she pulled the glass away from his mouth and set it on the bedside table. "I'll give you more in a moment. Or Jelsa will return with the tea."

He coughed as she laid him back on the pillow. Compared to the way his head ached and his bones felt as if they were freezing from the inside out, the pain of his wounds faded into the overall misery.

Once he'd regained his breath, he cracked his eyes open again. "My men. Are they all right?"

He should have asked the night before. If things hadn't been such a whirlwind, and if he hadn't been in such pain, he would have.

"They're alive. Yet until I'm queen, there's isn't much I can do." Adeline clasped her hands in her lap again. But she remained sitting at his side rather than moving. "It's bordering on treason having you here as it is."

Lorne grimaced, even as he gripped the blanket tighter. Here he was enjoying a soft, warm bed and the ministrations of both a princess and a physician while his loyal men remained in the dungeon, possibly still being tortured.

"I've already given the order to the guards I trust and to the physician to halt the torture and see to their wounds just as soon as my grandfather dies and I become queen." Adeline went back to staring at her hands rather than looking at him. "Hopefully my grandfather has been too preoccupied with dying and arranging my marriage to add any additional torture."

Lorne blinked at her, his sluggish brain struggling to figure out just what stood out to him in her words. "Your grandfather is arranging your marriage? But you're married to me?"

That last sentence shouldn't have come out a question. Yet the more the fogginess settled into his brain, the more he doubted his own memories of the previous night.

"I haven't exactly told my grandfather about you. I'd rather he die before ever finding out." Adeline's shoulders were hunching again, the slightest curve breaking her otherwise perfect posture. "I've bought time by claiming I'm taking time to think it over and examine the contract. But unless he takes a very sudden turn for the worse, he's going to push."

Despite his shivering, Lorne held out his hand to her again.

It was a long, aching moment before she glanced from his hand to his face and back to his hand. Then, as slowly as a skittish kitten, she reached out and rested her hand on his.

He curled his fingers around hers. They were so cold, or perhaps he was simply that feverish. "We are in this together. That's what we vowed last night, and I keep my vows."

She opened her mouth, but before she could speak, the door opened. Quick as a blink, she yanked her hand from his, returning it to rest demurely in her lap.

The physician and Jelsa entered with the tincture and tea things. As much as Lorne regretted the interruption, he wasn't going to regret the sweet oblivion of sleep the tincture would give him.

CHAPTER FIVE

Adeline stood by her grandfather's bedside, staring down at his still, dead form. After lingering for hours, the end had come mercifully and suddenly for a man who had caused so much pain to others.

Lord Sarlon turned to her, his hands clasped behind his back. He'd been the only lord allowed in to witness the king's death, a mark of how her grandfather had essentially begun handing the kingdom to him rather than her. "I need an answer on the betrothal. The kingdom should not be left without a monarch."

She didn't miss how he used the neutral *monarch* instead of *queen*. Lord Sarlon fully intended to make sure his son was the power behind the throne, not her.

The war for her crown had begun.

Despite her trembling hands and shaking knees, she kept her chin high, her back straight as she held

Lord Sarlon's gaze. "Please gather the council in the formal reception room. I will be there momentarily to make my marriage announcement."

A hint of a smile curved Lord Sarlon's mouth. He thought he had her cornered and that the marriage she'd be announcing would be the one to his son. "Very well, Highness."

He gave her a bow—the one for a princess, not yet the one for his queen—and left the room.

Adeline lingered another moment. In death, her grandfather was still and hollow, just a shell lacking the fire and power he exuded in life.

Yet even after death, he had the power to control her life. She would have to spend the first years of her reign undoing everything he'd done in the past decades.

If she survived the attempt.

With a deliberate spin on her heel, she strode from the room.

In the sitting room, the royal doctor lingered, as well as several of her grandfather's guards.

Adeline gestured from the doctor to the guards. "Please prepare his body for lying in state."

"Yes, Highness." The doctor and the guards gave bows before they strode past her into the king's bedchamber.

With that done, she left the king's suite and walked back to her rooms as quickly as she could without appearing to hurry.

Inside, her loyal guards, the physician, Jelsa, and

Thaddeus waited. All of them stood as she entered, and she swept a glance over them. "My grandfather, the king, is dead."

She should feel more emotion at those words. Something beyond this numb relief. He had been her last living relative, after all.

But being all alone in the world was better than having him for a grandfather.

Thaddeus dipped into a low bow. "Your Majesty. My queen."

The others followed, curtsying or bowing deeply.

Her heart ached. She was both honored and strangely melancholy at seeing her friends give her this deference.

"The council is convening in the reception room." Adeline glanced from Thaddeus to the physician. "Is Lord Lorne up for making an appearance?"

"No, but..." The physician shifted, as if he didn't think it was his place to say the rest out loud.

"He doesn't have much of a choice," Thaddeus finished in a quiet voice. "You need a husband standing beside you at the meeting."

"Yes, but I'll do my best to minimize how long he will have to stay." Adeline resisted the urge to glance at the bedchamber door. "Have him brought to the private waiting room."

"Very well, Majesty. I will see to him." The physician entered the bedchamber, followed by Thaddeus.

"Jelsa?" Adeline gestured down at her gray dress. "I will need to change into black."

"Of course, milady." Jelsa bobbed another curtsy. "I will also see to your hair. You will need to make a statement."

That she would. Adeline headed into the bedchamber, glancing only briefly at where the physician was checking on Lord Lorne's wounds and Thaddeus was laying out a new set of clothes, before she entered the dressing room.

In the dressing room, Adeline gave herself over to Jelsa's care. She dressed in one of the black dresses she had in her wardrobe before Jelsa set to work weaving another crown of braids, similar to what Adeline had worn for her late-night wedding, except that this time she tucked in diamond accents instead of pearls.

Adeline found herself physically ready long before she was mentally ready. All too soon, she was sweeping down the halls, Thaddeus just a step behind her and her guards trailing after, the physician's reassurance that he would have Lord Lorne in position still ringing in her ears.

She descended the stairs, strode down a short corridor, and halted before the double doors to the assembly hall. Only a few nights ago, she'd been married within this hall. Now she'd face down her council and hope they didn't revolt then and there.

The guards stationed there opened the door, and a footman called into the room, "Her Highness Princess Adeline."

The title was no longer correct, but the footman didn't know that.

As the occupants of the room stood and bowed in

her direction, Adeline glided inside, keeping her head high, the diamonds woven into the braid wound around her head winking in the light shining through the high windows. She didn't pause until she'd climbed the dais, where she turned and faced the gathered crowd of lords before her.

Her legs shook worse at the sight. So many men arrayed before her. Not a single ruling lady in sight since women couldn't inherit a title and sit on the council. It was amazing that Kelvernese law allowed women to inherit the throne at all.

Even if she couldn't inherit it without a man at her side. True, a man couldn't inherit without being married either. But she didn't think those marriages were as much about control as the men in this room intended hers to be.

Had she bypassed that domination? Or had she simply taken on another form of it by tying herself to the Lalsacian lord? She didn't know him well enough yet to see if he would be a man like her grandfather.

Or he could be a man like her father. Kind. Gentle. Self-sacrificing. Whatever confidence she still retained was a remnant of the love her father and mother had given her in her early years.

She wouldn't know for sure until Lord Lorne healed enough to no longer be so vulnerable and dependent.

Pushing the thoughts of Lord Lorne away, she faced the crowd of men packed into the rows of the hall. "King Jeraldo is dead."

She didn't even try to work up tears or a mourning

note to her voice. Right now, she was queen, and queens didn't have the luxury of emotions. Nor did she actually feel that sort of sorrow at her grandfather's passing.

Lord Axtol, the oldest lord on the council and therefore its head, stood. "As you know, the law clearly states that an heir to the crown must be married to ascend to the throne."

"If I might speak, Lord Axtol." Lord Sarlon slid to his feet as well, his expression as slick as his tone. When Lord Axtol nodded to him, Lord Sarlon held up a sheaf of papers. "Before he died, the late king negotiated a contract of betrothal between his granddaughter and my son. All it needs is the princess's signature to make it official."

Several of the lords leapt to their feet, shouting and protesting. Many of these lords also had eligible sons, and their protests had more to do with wanting to grab power by positioning their son as consort than any concern about her.

The few lords who were loyal to her remained seated and quiet, their gazes fixed on her as they waited for her to reveal the truth.

She let the commotion continue for several more minutes, forcing herself to note the various protests and sides the lords were taking. That would be important information for her to know going forward.

Near the door at the back of the room, Thaddeus lingered in the shadows. He, too, would be making the same notes, likely with far more political astuteness.

After another moment, she lifted a hand. "Silence, please."

It took long moments for the lords to quiet and retake their seats.

Her heart pounded harder as she looked out over the crowd. This was it. "Thank you for your concerns, gentlemen. But as it happens, I am already married."

After a heartbeat of stunned silence, most of the lords jumped to their feet again, the shouting and protesting starting up all over again. They were no more happy to have been denied their chance at the throne by her than they had been by Lord Sarlon.

This time, Adeline raised her hand and her voice right away, cutting them off. "Silence."

When the lords finally subsided to a semblance of calm, a low muttering still filled the hall.

Lord Sarlon faced her with barely contained fury suffusing his face. "To whom are you married?"

"To me." The new voice rang strong and confident behind Adeline from the direction of the door to the waiting room behind the dais. Bootsteps sounded on the flagstones before Lord Lorne appeared at her side. His head turned to her, his gaze meeting hers, as he held out his arm.

This close, she could see the brightness of fever in his eyes and the flush to his cheeks. But he was standing upright, dressed in a set of trousers, shirt, and doublet that fit him rather well.

While he didn't wear the Lalsacian colors, his black hair and darker colored skin were distinctive enough that there would be no mistaking who she had married.

She laid her hand on his arm, even as the lords before her burst into chaos once again.

"A Lalsacian!"

"You cannot be serious, Your Highness!"

"I will not stand for this!"

"How do we know this marriage is even real?"

Lord Pellier, one of the lords loyal to her, spoke for the first time, raising his voice. "The marriage is quite real. I witnessed it myself."

"Then you approve of this...travesty?" The other lord gestured to her and Lord Lorne.

"I believe this is our only path forward to peace with Lalsacia."

"Peace! Lalsacia just killed our king!"

"And we imprisoned their diplomatic envoys."

"They killed our crown prince and his princess before we were even at war! What we did to their envoys is nothing they didn't deserve!"

Beside her, Lord Lorne stiffened, but Adeline didn't dare glance at him. This moment was too precarious for any distraction, even if the words stabbed at her heart.

Forcing her emotions away, Adeline called for silence. The lords took far longer than any of the previous times to quiet, and the low murmurings continued. Most of the men before her had mutinous looks on their faces, and they remained standing instead of sitting.

"I understand your concern over my marriage.

There has been a lot of bloodshed and atrocities committed in this war." Adeline tried to keep her expression and voice neutral and stern. If she showed any weakness now, the lords would exploit it. "But my marriage signals both to you and to Lalsacia that I am resolved to bring about peace between Kelverny and Lalsacia, as is my husband Lord Lorne. It will be a long road, but I will see this through for the sake of our kingdom."

The lords stared at her, most of them appearing as if they were contemplating treason right then and there.

Her fingers tightened on Lord Lorne's arm, needing reassurance, even if the only one standing with her was the enemy lord she had married.

Surprisingly, his other hand came up to rest over hers on his arm. When she glanced at him, he gave her a hint of a smile and tilt of his head.

His support stiffened her spine and strengthened her voice as she stared out at her lords once again. "Since I am already married, I became queen the moment my grandfather breathed his last. Now I ask the council to recognize my right to rule."

Lord Pellier pressed his arm over his heart before he swept into a low bow. "My queen."

Others made the motion and bowed, holding the bow. Lord Sarlon and his ilk hesitated, but after a moment, they, too, bowed. Although Lord Sarlon did so with a sneer on his face. But even he was unwilling to make his move this publicly.

Not yet, anyway.

Adeline waited another heartbeat, letting them linger in their bows, before she motioned. "Rise."

The lords stood once again. After making a few final statements, Adeline gathered her skirts. A light pressure on Lord Lorne's arm had him turning in time with her before the two of them swept toward the door at the back of the dais. Lord Lorne remained a half-step behind her, even as they walked together, falling almost effortlessly into his role as consort.

He opened the door for her, and she stepped inside first. He followed, closing the door behind them.

Yet he didn't immediately move from the door, gripping the handle with white knuckles. His face had gone white, beads of sweat trickling down his temples.

"Come, you need to sit down." Adeline gripped him under the elbow, not sure if there was anything she could do if he couldn't manage to walk on his own.

The physician had pushed to his feet from the chair where he'd been waiting and was hurrying forward.

"I need to tell you...tell you..." Lord Lorne's voice was growing fainter as he swayed.

The physician arrived just in time to catch the Lalsacian as he collapsed.

"Is he all right?" Adeline still gripped Lord Lorne's arm, although she wasn't actually supporting any of his weight.

The physician pressed his hand to Lord Lorne's forehead, his brow furrowed. "His fever is spiking. He needs to be back in bed and resting."

Adeline nodded. Lord Lorne had pushed himself

beyond what he should have to stand at her side back there.

Hopefully he hadn't pushed himself too hard. Strangely, she didn't want to find herself a widow before she even had the chance to get to know this Lalsacian lord she'd married.

CHAPTER SIX

Adeline stood beside the casket where her grandfather was laid out in his royal finery. Her skin crawled as she forced herself to stand tall and smile serenely at those filing past her to pay their respects. With each person, she was all too aware of her own vulnerability. It would be far too easy for one of them to leap forward with knife in hand.

At her back, the guards she trusted had been joined by others among the royal guard. After all, her loyal guards couldn't be on duty all the time. They needed sleep and rest.

But who among those guards were loyal to her, or at the very least, loyal enough to the crown that they wouldn't turn on her? Would they bother to stop an assassin if someone tried to kill her?

On the other side of the coffin, Lord Axtol and Lord Sarlon stood as representatives of the council. Yet even after paying their respects, many of the nobles lingered in the room. All of them assessing her.

How many were already plotting? How many would support her bid to bring about peace and how many would wish to see her dead because of it?

Her fingers trembled, and she clasped her hands in front of her.

If only she didn't have to stand alone. If only she had someone to remain at her side in moments like this.

But Jelsa was a mere maid and had remained in Adeline's rooms. Thaddeus, too, was a commoner, a lowly steward.

Her mind flashed to Lord Lorne and that moment when he'd stood beside her before the council when she'd announced that she was married. The solidness of his arm beneath her hand had been so steady, his presence so reassuring. For a brief moment, she hadn't felt alone for the first time since her parents died.

Yet Lord Lorne was currently lying in her bed, out of his head with fever. He hadn't woken since his collapse the day before.

Besides, he was an enemy. Regardless of their shared wish for peace between their kingdoms, she shouldn't count him as a true ally. He could turn on her just as easily as everyone else.

At last, the hours of her ceremonial vigil ended. Yet even then, she wasn't free to retreat.

First, she had to meet with the council, where she was pummeled on all sides by the various lords pushing their agendas. Even those who were technically loyal to her looked at her with resignation, as if they supported her because they were loyal to the crown, but they didn't truly think she was strong enough to rule the kingdom.

Finally, she settled behind the desk in the king's study and stared listlessly at the stacks of paperwork before her. Where should she start?

A knock sounded on the door before Thaddeus stepped inside. He took one look at her before he closed the door softly behind him. "Are you all right, Your Majesty?"

"No." She hated how tiny her voice was. She peered up at Thaddeus. "I can't do this. No one believes I can do this."

"*I* believe you can." Thaddeus stepped forward before he knelt on one knee, his arm over his chest in the royal salute. "So do many others. We have seen your courage as you survived your grandfather. You will survive this too."

Survive. There was so little joy in that word. Survive merely meant get through the day. It didn't mean happiness. It didn't mean smiles and laughter and all the things she'd lost when she'd lost her parents.

Perhaps survival was all she could expect out of her life.

"Thank you." She didn't feel better, but she forced herself to smile and gather herself anyway. Thaddeus would do his best to support her, as he always did. But there was a gulf between them that he couldn't cross.

For some reason, that brought Lord Lorne to her mind once again.

"How is Lord Lorne?" Adeline focused on the stacks

of paperwork, even as Thaddeus tottered back to his feet.

"Still out with fever." Thaddeus's face remained grave, etched with deep grooves. "The physician is concerned. If the fever doesn't break soon…"

Then she would lose him and the shield from the lords that he provided. She'd lose her link to Lalsacia and the potential of peace with that kingdom.

And she'd lose one ally who might be able to stand with her as a partner.

Straightening her shoulders, she gestured at the paperwork. "Help me gather the most important papers. I'm going to deal with this in my room."

He drifted on waves of heat, even as ice wracked his bones. At times, he grew aware of voices near him. Cups of water and tea were pressed to his lips, even as the hazy voices urged him to drink.

Sometimes, lines of pain cut across his back and chest. He cried out and thrashed, yet hands pinned him down firmly.

He wasn't sure how much time passed before he dragged himself toward true wakefulness. He blinked gummy eyelids, an orange light suffused around him.

When he had gathered his strength, he turned his head, first one way to take in the rest of the room, then the other way to glance at the far side of the bed.

Queen Adeline sat there, her legs under the blankets, her back to the headboard. She had a lap desk spread with papers, and her gaze was currently focused on one of them. Her lips moved as she read, as if she didn't realize she was murmuring to herself, while her brow was furrowed.

He licked his lips, trying to find enough saliva to get his tongue to work. "Good morning. Or is it good afternoon?"

She started, jumping so high she nearly tipped over the lap desk. She grabbed the inkpot before it toppled. "You scared me."

"Sorry." Lorne tried to lift his hand, but he was too weak to disentangle his arm from the blankets.

"No, no, don't apologize. I'm glad to see you awake." She placed the inkpot on the table before she set the whole lap desk on the end of the bed past her feet. "I should fetch the physician."

This time, he managed to free his hand, and he grabbed hers before she could climb off the bed. "Not yet."

She halted, her legs off the side of the bed, her other hand gripping the blankets. "Are you sure? You were out for a day and a half. We were all rather concerned."

He could feel the clammy stickiness of sweat all over him, but the bone-wracking cold was finally gone.

"Just a few more minutes." He couldn't explain why he wanted these minutes with her before the physician arrived and started poking and prodding. "Could I have some water?"

"Yes, of course." She hurried to fetch the glass and pour the water from the pitcher, as she'd done before.

This time when she held the glass to his mouth, he was able to drain the glass, the water filling his stomach and soothing his dry mouth.

As she returned the glass to the table, he struggled to push himself more upright on the pillow. His ribs stabbed pain through his chest, and weakness trembled through his limbs. But the fog in his mind had mostly disappeared.

Turning from the table, Adeline paused, her gaze flicking from him to her hands for a moment, before she returned to sit on the far edge of the bed, nowhere near as comfortably perched as she had been before.

"My men?" He searched her face, her posture, the tight line of her mouth.

"They've been taken out of the dungeon and are recovering in a suite of guest rooms down the hall." Adeline's fingers twisted together in her lap. "The physician has tended them. They have similar injuries to yours, but they seem to be recovering well. None of them show signs of the fever that gripped you."

"Thank you." He released a sigh and closed his eyes for a moment. His men were no longer in the dungeon. They would be fine. He hadn't gotten them all killed with his ill-advised bid for peace.

At least, not yet. He opened his eyes and peered at Adeline. He was now partway into another bid for peace, although only time would tell if this one was as ill-advised as his last one.

He held out his hand toward her, although he wasn't quite sure why. It wasn't like he expected her to take it. But reaching for her seemed like the right thing to do. "How are you holding up?"

"Not well." She drew her knees up before hugging them. "It's all so much, and everyone expects me to fail, including many of those who are loyal to me. And there are so many who aren't loyal. I'm just...scared."

He kept his hand out there between them, offering that comfort if she wanted it. "I don't blame you. No one should be as alone and isolated as you are in your own kingdom. But I'm here for you. You aren't alone."

As she had before, she tentatively placed her hand on his, her gaze meeting his.

After another moment, she withdrew her hand and stood. "I should fetch the physician."

He supposed he couldn't delay any longer.

LORNE RESTED IN A COMFORTABLE CHAIR IN THE SITTING room of the suite connected to Adeline's.

At least he was up for the first time since he'd collapsed. With the help from a footman whom Jelsa had recommended as trustworthy, he'd tottered from Adeline's room to this suite. Despite the way the soap stung in his wounds, he'd enjoyed his first bath since he'd been taken from the dungeon. The physician had come again to rebandage him, then the footman had helped him dress in clean clothes that didn't reek of his own sweat.

After taking a short nap since just that much

activity had worn him out, he'd rallied his strength to sit here, waiting just out of sight of the door.

There came a knock on his door before it opened without waiting for him to call out. One of the guards stood to the side while the others motioned for the group of men they escorted to enter the room.

Their stances stiff, their bodies poised for action, five men strode into the room, glancing around warily.

As the first man's gaze landed on Lorne, he halted so abruptly that the others piled into him. He staggered but kept his feet, even as he gaped.

"What—" One of the others began to speak before he, too, spotted Lorne. He rushed over, dropping to his knees before Lorne. "Your—"

Lorne shook his head, holding out a hand to halt Orvyn before he said anything out loud.

As if remembering himself, Orvyn clamped his mouth shut, even as he remained kneeling before Lorne.

Once the guards closed the door, leaving them alone, the others hurried closer, even as their eyes remained wide.

Godwin, a gray-haired man with dark brown eyes set in a weathered face, knelt next to Orvyn and bowed his head. "Sir. It is good to see you alive. We thought... we were told..."

"When they didn't bring you back, we feared the worst." Burchard, his brown hair also peppered with gray, spoke in a choked tone as he knelt beside Godwin. "Then the guards told us you were dead. They taunted us with it. They knew how we would despair."

Lorne squeezed his eyes shut for a moment. He should have asked Adeline to send word that he was alive. But he'd been out of his mind with fever, and she'd been busy with becoming queen. He was honored that she'd even remembered her promise to release his men as soon as she could.

But he should have remembered them. He should have guessed that the guards wouldn't tell them the truth.

"I'm sorry I didn't send word. And that I wasn't able to get you out of the dungeon sooner." Lorne opened his eyes, taking in the men before him. Godwin and Burchard, the oldest among the royal guards assigned to him. Arne and Emil, the two strongest among his guards. And Orvyn, a young man around his age. When he had been assigned to Lorne's guards, he had become a good friend. "I'm thankful you are all right. I was worried."

While they bore the bruises and bandages of their time in the dungeon, they were moving far easier than he was.

"What happened, sir?" Godwin remained kneeling before him, as if he couldn't bring himself to move.

"Please, sit. It will take some explanation." Lorne gestured to the other couches and chairs in the room.

His men slowly took seats, their eyes still fixed on him as if they didn't dare look away.

"That day, I was brought to the torture room. But instead of torture, Princess Adeline of Kelverny waited there." Lorne picked his words carefully, his stomach clenching. The Kelvernese guards were likely listening at the door, and he couldn't guarantee all of them were loyal to Adeline. But he was also strangely nervous about telling his men what he'd done. "She had a proposal for me. She wanted to marry me."

"What?" Both Arne and Emil surged to their feet, their mouths hanging open.

Burchard grimaced, and Godwin eyed Lorne rather grimly. Only Orvyn grinned as he met Lorne's gaze. "I'm guessing you said yes?"

"Of course I said yes." Lorne waved toward the connecting door. "She wished to marry me in order to help bring about peace between our kingdoms. As I'm also committed to peace, it seemed a good way to achieve our mutual goal."

"But does she…" Returning to his seat, Arne eyed first the connecting door, then the outer door, before he leaned closer, his voice going so low it barely carried even to Lorne. "Does she know who you are?"

"No. No one does." Lorne met Arne's gaze. "And they must not find out. Not until peace has been achieved."

"Yes, of course. But, sir, are you sure this was a good idea?" Godwin leaned his elbows on his knees as he searched Lorne's face. "The political ramifications…"

"I know. It's going to be complicated." Lorne waved his hand again. "But it might be the only way to gain peace."

"Is it, though?" Emil glanced around at each of them, lowering his voice. "I hate to suggest it, but he's now rather uniquely positioned to, uh, end the Kelvernese royal line."

Just hearing those words was a punch to Lorne's chest. He was shaking his head vigorously before he'd even put much thought behind the gesture. "No."

"You have to admit, it would be one quick way to solve our problems." Emil shrugged.

"I've had the chance to get a better feel for the political situation here." Lorne tried to keep his voice level. Logical. "If Queen Adeline were killed, the warmongering lords would be the ones positioned to take over. They would continue the war, and they'd use the death of their queen to call for blood, just as they did with the deaths of their crown prince and princess five years ago. Killing her would only make our situation worse, not end the war."

"I see." Emil nodded, bowing his head slightly. "Then should we escape? We have a better chance, now that we aren't in the dungeon."

Lorne shook his head again, although without the frantic vigor of a moment ago. He couldn't leave his wife to fend for herself against all that was arrayed against her right now. "No. Leaving will just put us right back where we started."

"Then what are your orders, sir?" Orvyn's smile tipped slightly, his eyes twinkling, as if he'd already guessed what those orders would be.

"We need to keep Queen Adeline alive." Lorne met each of their gazes, not looking away until he saw agreement written there. "She's Lalsacia's only chance for peace. But right now, her position is tenuous. She has far more lords plotting against her than she has on her side. And as we know, Kelverny is not above assassinating their own to perpetuate this war."

That was something he had yet to tell Adeline. He had been about to, before he'd collapsed.

But he had to tell her. Soon. No matter how much the words would wreck her.

"Very well, sir." Godwin bowed from the waist from where he sat. "We will do our best to keep both of you safe. But you are still our priority."

Lorne nodded. If his men suspected that he was in too much danger, they would smuggle him out of Kelverny and back to Lalsacia without any care for who he might be leaving behind.

CHAPTER SEVEN

Sitting on her bed, Adeline bent over her lap desk, her eyes burning at the late hour. The low lamplight cast orange light and dark shadows across her room and across the page, even as the words swam before her.

All this paperwork. She'd known there would be a lot as queen, but it almost seemed that the Council was piling it on to put her even more off-balance than she already was. Their means of exerting control over her and proving that she wasn't fit to be queen.

For things like tax records and payments and military numbers, there was a team of stewards and assistants who oversaw those things. They were her grandfather's loyal men, but Thaddeus was also pulling late hours—later hours than he should at his age—to double-check their numbers to ensure none of them were trying to cheat the crown in some way.

But for everything else, she was essentially on her own. The current sheaf before her contained petitions from the nobility. Lord Lerroy wanted royal funds to repair a bridge over a river. Lord Avery wanted a larger allotment of royal grain to supply a village after a blight killed the crops. But Lord Fellton was arguing that the troops at the border needed every bit of grain and that the villagers would just have to fend for themselves.

Even if things appeared somewhat straightforward on the surface, there was the secondary level of politics behind everything. Yes, that bridge over the river sounded like it was in desperate need of repair. Someone could get hurt if it wasn't. But if she approved the bridge for Lord Lerroy, then Lord Harding would see it as favoritism and protest, wanting her to also approve road improvements near his estate, even though those road improvements were nowhere near as necessary.

How was she to wade through all of this? If her parents had lived, her father would likely have taken her to meetings and started training her for this long before now.

But her grandfather had kept her far from all of that, and she'd had no power to protest being shut out. He'd wanted her to be ignorant and pliable so that he could marry her to someone who would follow in his footsteps, like Lord Sarlon's son.

Thanks to her grandfather, she was now woefully unprepared. He'd ensured she would fail, even after she'd thwarted his plans to marry her off.

A knock made her jump and nearly tip her inkpot over yet again. Perhaps working on a lap desk in her bed wasn't the best idea, even if she preferred hiding here rather than working in her study.

She lifted her head, looking first to the door to the sitting room. But that door remained closed, no one in sight.

When she turned her head, the connecting door between bedchambers stood open, and Lord Lorne leaned against the jamb, not quite stepping inside.

Her stomach gave a flip. She'd been somewhat relieved and yet strangely disappointed when she'd readied for bed, only to find it empty. But of course, now that he could shuffle around, he would choose to sleep in the adjoining room. His men were bedding down in his sitting room rather than returning to their own suite of rooms in order to set up a better guard over him.

Besides, now that he was healed enough to get up and walk, he could be as much a danger to her as everyone else she didn't fully trust. She shouldn't miss his presence. She definitely shouldn't see him as safe enough to leave the door between their bedchambers unlocked.

Too bad her heart didn't quite agree.

"I'm sorry to disturb you." Lord Lorne dipped his head for a moment before raising it again, meeting her gaze with a searching look of his own. "I considered sleeping in the other room, but I thought it might be wiser for us to stay together. No reason for our guards to protect two rooms when they can pool their resources and guard only one. And you'll be safer with someone here to protect you."

She stared at him, frozen at the sight of him upright, clean, and looking rather handsome with his dark hair and duskier skin tone, shades darker than her pallor.

It was one thing to have him in her bed when he'd been unconscious and injured to the point of immobility. But it was another thing entirely to *invite* him to share her bed. He was still healing, still hunching slightly with his broken ribs. But he was far from immobile or incapable now.

Heat rose in her cheeks. "I...uh..."

"I promise, I will not cross any of your boundaries." He remained where he was, as if he wouldn't so much as step a toe across the threshold until she gave her permission. "All I'm going to do is sleep. And protect you should an assassin make it past our guards."

"Do you think an assassin is likely?" The word *assassin* sent her hands shaking more than the thought of him joining her in bed.

"Sadly, yes." Lord Lorne still didn't enter the room. He was leaning more heavily against the jamb, and he moved one arm to wrap over his stomach. While he looked more hale and healthy, he was far from strong. Just standing for that long had his face paling, his breathing growing heavier. "Although, the assassin could just as easily be for me as for you. After all, I'm the one standing in the way of you marrying a lord's son of the council's choice."

"Then having you here could put me at even more risk, not less." She twisted her hands in the blankets, her heart hammering harder in her throat. Despite her protests, her skin crawled at the thought of being in this room alone, sleeping and vulnerable, now that he'd mentioned the probability of an assassination.

"Perhaps." Lord Lorne grimaced, although the expression could have been because of his growing pain as much as the topic. "But anyone who sends an assassin after me might consider it just as easy to have the assassin kill both of us while he's at it. Yes, sleeping in the same room will make it easier for the assassin. But it won't split our guards' response, especially since those we know are loyal are so few. I'll have a chance of fighting back, once I'm more healed, of course."

Lord Lorne shouldn't feel safe. He was an enemy lord, only bound to her by their tenuous marriage vows and their shared desire for peace. He could even be using the excuse of protecting her as a means to get close enough to kill her himself.

Yet he'd offered comfort. Safety. A listening ear. A hand to hold. And that was all in the few hours he'd been lucid. He'd given her more warmth and care than her grandfather ever had.

And now he was offering to essentially be her bodyguard while she slept.

Her fingers clutching the edge of the lap desk, she managed a nod. "Yes. Please come in. Come..."

She couldn't manage to finish, her face burning. She couldn't look at him as he crossed the room with soft steps, the bed dipping under his weight as he sat on the other side. Instead, she busied herself with setting aside her lap desk and paperwork. When she didn't have anything else to fiddle with, she buried her fingers in the blankets.

Her skin prickled with awareness of him, her breath catching in her throat. He was so close, and she was so vulnerable. Vulnerable to him. Vulnerable to the council. Vulnerable to a potential assassin. It seemed all she managed to be was vulnerable and scared. Hardly the strong queen her kingdom needed.

The blankets shifted as he tucked his legs beneath them, although he didn't lie down. Instead he remained sitting against the headboard as she was doing.

After a moment, he placed his hand on the bed between them, palm up. Extending the offer, but not presuming to simply take her hand. When she glanced at him, he gave her a small, slightly lopsided smile. "Just sleep. I promise."

Maybe she shouldn't believe the truth in his voice and sincerity in his eyes. Perhaps she was truly as weak as Lord Sarlon and most of the council believed.

But she untangled one of her hands from the blankets and grasped his hand, squeezing tightly even before he closed his fingers around hers. She needed someone to hold on to, and it turned out that this enemy lord was her only choice.

His smile widened, his posture easing slightly. But instead of looking at her, he rested his head against the headboard, tipping his head back as he closed his eyes. "If you are amiable, I was thinking we should randomly switch sleeping in here and sleeping in the other room. We'll let our most trusted guards know which room we'll be in, but no one else. Not even the other guards stationed in the corridor. A few minutes of trying to find which room we're in could buy us crucial seconds in the case of an assassination attempt."

"A good precaution." Adeline peeked at him. "How dangerous is the Lalsacian court that you think of these things?"

"Far less dangerous than the Kelvernese court, I assure you." Lord Lorne's eyes remained closed. "But we've had reason to fear assassins sent from Kelverny."

Oh. Right. She would have said her kingdom wouldn't do such a thing, but she wouldn't put anything past her grandfather. He had, after all, arrested and tortured diplomatic envoys who had been under the flag of truce.

"About assassins..." Lord Lorne's posture tensed, and he lifted his head once again. When he met her gaze, there was something compassionate and aching in his eyes. "I have something to tell you. About your parents. I meant to tell you long before now. After all, it's the reason I organized the diplomatic mission. I thought this information might make a difference to relations between our kingdoms."

"What? What about my parents?" She tucked her knees tighter to her chest, wrapping her free arm around them. Her other hand gripped his so tightly that it had to hurt, but he didn't pull away.

"There were no Lalsacian units in that area of the pass the day your parents were killed." Lord Lorne held her gaze with unwavering intensity.

"No." She shook her head, as if she could forcibly expel his words from her ears. "No, it's not possible. I'm sure it was a mistake. Your kingdom didn't mean to kill them. But…"

"I know I don't have any proof that I can show you." Lord Lorne's fingers flexed around hers, but his gaze remained locked on her. "But I talked to every Lalsacian commander who was stationed in the pass that day. I talked to as many of the soldiers as I could track down. I searched our military records and confirmed everything with my…king. Lalsacia did not kill your parents."

"No." Her protest came out weaker than before.

She didn't want to believe it. Her parents' deaths had been her grandfather's whole excuse for the war. It had been his reason for capturing and torturing Lord Lorne and his men.

If Lalsacia didn't kill her parents, then that only left…

"Surely my grandfather wouldn't have killed his own son. He was his heir." She was still shaking her head, although slower, her shoulders hunching. She'd just been thinking that she wouldn't put anything past her grandfather. But this?

"Not his only heir." Lord Lorne eyed her. "He had one other heir. One he believed he could control and mold and eventually marry off to the son of his crony to further control her."

"No, he wouldn't…" She trailed off, curling in on herself. Her father had been vocal against any plans to go to war with Lalsacia. He'd rallied the lords opposed to war, and he'd been the leading voice standing against her grandfather.

Her grandfather had used that stance to force her father to prove how much he wanted peace with Lalsacia by going on that diplomatic mission, and taking her mother with him.

"It's possible it wasn't your grandfather." Lord Lorne squeezed her hand. "Lord Sarlon would be my other top suspect. He certainly leveraged your father's absence to worm his way into being your grandfather's right-hand man. And he'd positioned his son to become king one day."

"Or they worked together." She wasn't sure which option was better or worse.

"Or that." Lord Lorne nodded, his jaw set. "After all, your grandfather didn't personally carry out the raid. He worked with someone to commit the actual murders, if he's the one responsible."

"Do you think we could find proof? In my grandfather's things or Lord Sarlon's?" If this was true, then she needed proof. She needed to *know* exactly who had done this to her parents.

"I highly doubt either of them left a paper trail. Any orders were given in person." Lord Lorne shook his head on a sigh. "If they were especially cautious, then those who carried out the deed were also killed shortly afterwards. There might be no witnesses alive, and if your grandfather was solely behind it, then he took the full truth to his grave."

"But if Lord Sarlon was involved, either as my grandfather's man or acting on his own, then he knows the truth." Adeline's stomach churned, yet a burning feeling filled her chest.

"He'd have to confess, and you'd need a great deal of persuasion to get him to talk." Lord Lorne rubbed his thumb over the back of her hand. "But, Adeline, if Lord Sarlon is involved in any way, then it means that he has participated in the assassination of his royal family before. He won't hesitate to do it again to achieve his goals."

"That's why you're so worried that I'll be a target of assassination attempts, not just you." She curled tighter on the bed. She'd known she was a target, but this discussion made it all more real.

"Yes." Lord Lorne breathed the word on another sigh. "I think you'll be reasonably safe for a while. After all, the easiest path for Lord Sarlon is still to have you marry his son. A full-on coup gets messy and doesn't guarantee success. So I'll be his primary target since he needs me out of the way first. But if he can rally enough support, he might go for the radical option and do away with you entirely, placing himself rather than his son on the throne. If he's as power-hungry as he seems, then that option would have a certain appeal."

Assassination. Scheming lords. Murder.

Adeline shook as she tried to absorb it. Her parents had been murdered. Not just killed by an enemy. Not killed in a tragic accident at the border. But murdered, either by her grandfather or Lord Sarlon or both.

"I...I..." She was going to cry. Or scream. She wasn't sure what to do with the pain building in her chest.

Lord Lorne held out his free arm in an invitation.

She let go of his other hand long enough to tuck herself against him, her head on his shoulder. His arms came around her, holding her close. When she wrapped her arms around his waist, he hissed and flinched.

"Sorry." She began to shift away from him.

"Just the ribs. Here." He let go of her long enough to adjust her grip on him. "That's better."

She closed her eyes and, finally, let herself cry.

CHAPTER EIGHT

Lorne strode down the corridor as steadily as he could manage, surrounded by three of his guards and three Kelvernese guards who were among those Adeline trusted.

He'd regained some of his strength in the past two days, but he was nowhere near back to fighting ready. Not that he'd ever been the warrior that his guards were, but he'd been able to hold his own before all this happened.

Partway down the corridor, three guards stood outside a door. One of the guards even had a gray-and-black-striped sylon cat on a leash at his side, the cat poised, its tail twitching. The white ruff around its neck showed that it was male while its paws and the end of the tail were also fringed in white. While sitting, the cat's head came up to the guard's waist.

Lorne forced himself not to shudder at the sight of the huge war cat, the wounds across his stomach twinging with the memory of a similar cat slashing him open with its claws.

When he halted at the door, the cat didn't give him more than a cursory glance before it began licking one of its front paws. He dragged his head up and pretended he wasn't unsettled. "Lord Lorne to see the queen."

He was, officially, the prince consort now, and he probably should have used the title prince. But that felt too dangerous, too close to his real identity. Better to remain unassuming.

The guard closest to the door nodded and stepped even more aside. "The queen gave orders that you are always to be admitted."

Lorne breathed out a sigh of relief. He hadn't been sure, when he'd set out from their rooms, that he'd be allowed to set foot here.

He pushed the door open and stepped inside, followed by several of his guards. He hadn't heard them consult, but somehow they'd split off, leaving two in the corridor and three inside here with him.

He found himself in a small sitting room, the comfortable chairs arranged as if to disguise the fact that this was essentially an area to wait to have a private audience with the monarch. The colors were done in dark woods and dark reds, highlighted with gaudy golds. Definitely Adeline's grandfather's style rather than hers.

Six other guards, including two of his men, already packed into the room, standing near the walls. His men gave him slight nods.

Across the way, another door stood open. Raised voices rang from inside, accompanied by the pounding of a fist.

"We need this bridge! It's a safety hazard!"

"If he gets funds, then the roads in my district should be funded too!"

"The roads in your district are just fine!"

With each sentence, the men's voices grew even louder. The guards on either side of the door glanced at each other, as if wondering if they should intervene.

But they didn't have the clout to interrupt two lords.

Lorne did.

He marched across the room and strode into the office on the far side as steadily as he could manage.

Inside, two lords he vaguely recognized from the gathering of the council he'd attended loomed over Adeline's desk. One even had the temerity to press his palms to the surface and lean forward, as if to intimidate his queen.

Adeline sat sword-straight in her chair, her chin high, but he could see the way she was barely holding herself together. Her hands were hidden beneath the desk, but he'd bet they were trembling. As he entered, her gaze flicked up to his, something like a desperate pleading for rescue in those brown depths.

How to rescue her without undermining her position as queen? Or without seeming to wield too much authority for a man from an enemy kingdom?

"What is he doing here?" One of the lords sneered over his shoulder at Lorne.

The other didn't speak, but he had a similar look of disgust curling his mouth.

Lorne plastered on a smile and added a slight saunter to his gait as he edged around the two men. "I apologize for the interruption, but I simply had to have a moment with my lovely wife."

"He is my husband. I gave him permission to interrupt anytime." Adeline didn't quite manage as nonchalant a tone as he had, but she didn't flinch when he bent down and pressed a light kiss to her cheek.

Perhaps the gesture was crossing a line, but it put his mouth close enough to her ear for him to whisper, "I'm here. Tell me what you need."

She gave the slightest nod in response, her hands twitching in her lap.

He would have liked to reach down and take one, but he didn't dare demonstrate that much affection with the two lords watching. Instead, he took a spot at her shoulder and just slightly behind her, as befitted his standing as consort. When he rested his hand on the back of her chair, his fingers just brushed her shoulder in what he hoped was a comforting touch.

Some of her shaking stilled, and when she faced the two lords again, she had a new steel in her eyes and in her voice. "I have made my decision, gentlemen. The bridge in Eldenville is a hazard and must be fixed. But, Lord Harding, the roads in Durry are currently adequate. The royal funds are better spent elsewhere at this time. However, should the war end, freeing up more royal funding, I will consider the roads in Durry as high on the list for allocating those funds."

The lords finally bowed and left, one with a triumphant stride and the other with jaw still working. A guard shut the door after them, leaving Adeline and Lorne alone.

Adeline gusted out a sigh, shuddered, and slumped over her desk. "I can't do this. I was about to burst into tears before you came in."

Lorne stepped to her side and knelt so that he was looking up at her rather than her craning her neck to see him. "I thought you handled that well. Clever to put in a mention of how ending the war will benefit the kingdom. If that lord feels strongly enough about his roads, he might consider backing you when you pursue peace with Lalsacia."

"I hope so. Or he will be so angry with me that he will oppose anything I do, no matter how sensible." Adeline glanced at him before swinging her despairing gaze back to the piles of paperwork on her desk. "I've sent word to the troops at the border to stand down and only defend themselves if Lalsacia attacks, but things haven't deescalated enough to reach out yet."

"Perhaps if I wrote a letter? You could send it with a trusted emissary. Or one of my men." Lorne worked to keep his tone casual, as if this didn't matter a great deal to him.

He didn't dare write his father outright that he was alive. But his father would recognize his handwriting, and if he could convince Adeline to send one of his guards, that guard could tell his father in person what had happened.

Adeline paused, considering, before she shook her

head. "I'd like to make our more peaceful stance clear by our lack of attacks at the border before making any overtures of peace. After what my grandfather did to you and your men, Lalsacia's king might do the same to any envoys I send. And I'd rather your king not find out exactly what my grandfather did to you and your men until after a peace is signed, so I can't send one of your men or even a letter just yet."

From her standpoint, such a thing would make sense. She wouldn't want to enrage the Lalsacian king with news of torture before presenting him with a peace treaty. Nor did she fully trust him yet. She didn't dare allow him to write a letter that might have a code hidden in it somewhere.

She didn't know that the Lalsacian king was his father. Lorne could smooth the way for her and for peace, despite what had happened. While he might add a code to a letter, he'd only do it to reassure his father that he was alive and well.

Yet unless he wanted to confess the truth, he couldn't argue with her decision, painful as it was to leave his father still worried, still wondering. Did his father assume that he was dead? Did he know that Lorne had been captured and brought back to Kelverny?

What else could he do but acquiesce and bide his time, waiting for an opportunity to send word to his father?

"All right. I understand." Lorne pushed to his feet, rounded the desk, and sank into one of the chairs facing her, stifling his groan at the way his ribs still hurt. He gestured at the stacks of paperwork. "If I were a normal prince consort, I'd be able to help you with this."

"But you're from an enemy kingdom." Adeline's mouth tipped with the first hint of a smile since he'd come in. "I'm afraid I can't allow you to see sensitive documents."

"No." Lorne regarded the piles. If he didn't help her in some way, she'd never finish. "But you could talk the less sensitive stuff over with me. Like that whole thing with the bridge and the roads. I can be your sounding board. I do, after all, have some experience with government."

He couldn't tell her just how much experience. Far more than a lowly lord would have. But even a normal lord in Lalsacia would have a good idea of politics and how the government worked.

Adeline's smile widened, her posture straightening, although with less tension than when she'd been facing the two lords. "That would be wonderful. Perhaps I wouldn't have this overwhelming sense I'm doing everything wrong and going to fail if I can talk the decisions over with someone."

"You are *not* going to fail." Since Lorne sat across the desk from her, he didn't hold out his hand. But he held her gaze for a long moment before he waved a hand at the papers. "Where would you like to start?"

"This stack." She grabbed the largest of the stacks, sliding it toward her rather than picking it up. At his look, her smile took on a wry tilt. "I sorted the paperwork by category. This is all the various requests from nobles, towns, merchants, etc. While Thaddeus can assist me with tax stuff and I can't show you anything regarding the war, there shouldn't be any problem talking over the items in this stack with you."

"Then let's get started." Lorne grinned and eased deeper onto the cushioned seat, careful of his healing ribs.

As frustrated as he was by not being able to send a message to his father, he needed to be patient. Gaining Adeline's trust would go a lot farther in ending this war and bringing about real peace than pushing too hard now.

⚭

ADELINE TOOK IN HER DESK AND THE STACK OF FINISHED paperwork. Thanks to Lorne's help, she'd gone through the whole pile of requests and either approved or rejected them, giving solid reasoning for each. There were those who would still complain about her decisions, but at least she felt more confident in them after talking everything over with Lorne.

That left only one small matter she had to take care of. With a glance at Lorne's seat, now empty since she'd sent him to rest, she pulled out a fresh sheet of paper.

It took her some time to craft the right words. Despite what she'd told Lord Lorne, she intended to send a letter to the Lalsacian king.

She didn't want to promise anything or mention too much about Lalsacia's envoys, but she also needed to make this first gesture of peace. Kelverny had been behind this whole war—from her parents' deaths to the latest atrocities committed against Lord Lorne and his men—and thus the burden of peace rested on her.

As she was finishing up, there was a knock on her door. When she called out for the person to enter, Thaddeus stepped inside. He bowed. "I've finished going over the audit with the clerks and accountants. The castle finances, at least, appear to be in order."

"Thank you, Thaddeus." She gestured at the chair across from her. "I appreciate all the extra work you've been taking on."

He really should be contemplating retirement, not pulling even longer hours.

"It's my pleasure, Your Majesty." Thaddeus eased himself into the chair, a grimace betraying him. His knees must be hurting him. "And it has been encouraging, talking to more of the castle staff. There is hope in their eyes. They are beginning to believe in you, and that will go a long way toward gaining their loyalty."

"I hope so." She dropped her gaze to the paper before her, drew a deep breath, and pushed it toward him. "Could you please read this over?"

Thaddeus took the paper, his thinning gray eyebrows raising as he read the first few lines. But he read the whole thing without comment and stared at it for a long moment before he lowered it to look at her over it. "This is well written."

"You think so?" She twisted her hands together in her lap.

"Yes. Diplomatic but to the point. Admitting

Kelverny's wrongdoing in the war without groveling or lowering our dignity." Thaddeus regarded her over the top of the paper. "But you don't mention your marriage to Lord Lorne?"

"No." She couldn't fully explain her reluctance to mention it nor to have Lord Lorne involved in the peace process. Peace had been the reason she married him, after all.

But she didn't want to use him as a bargaining chip. Nor did she want to trap him. He'd been in an impossible situation, and she'd given him the options of more torture or marriage. That was hardly a choice.

And if she used him as her pawn for bringing about peace, he would remain trapped in marriage to her.

It hadn't bothered her that she was using him before. But now that she knew him...now that holding his hand strengthened her in a way nothing else had before...she couldn't do that to him. She wanted him to choose her. Not for peace. Not for their kingdoms. But for her.

Foolishness, she knew. Neither of them would ever have that kind of freedom. But perhaps she could spare him, somewhat.

Thaddeus was still looking at her, as if waiting for her to elaborate. She drew her shoulders straighter. "I'd like to hold off on mentioning Lord Lorne or our connection just yet. That can be an additional bargaining tool if we need it. My grandfather's treatment of Lord Lorne and his men was abominable, and admitting that won't do our bid for peace any favors right now."

"I see." Thaddeus spoke the words slowly, the look in his eyes saying that he, indeed, saw far more than she wanted him to see.

Adeline took the paper from him, signed and sealed it, rolled it, and sealed it again. Only then did she hand it back to him. "Could you please ensure this is handed off to an officer we can trust? Give him instructions to approach the Lalsacian lines only after the tensions are cooled enough that he thinks he will be heard under a flag of truce instead of filled full of arrows on sight."

"Yes, Your Majesty." Thaddeus tucked the roll of paper into an inner pocket of his jacket before he stood and bowed.

As he left, Adeline released a long sigh. It would be weeks before she heard anything in reply from the Lalsacian king. It might take the officer weeks to dare approach the Lalsacians, then weeks more before the enemy king sent a reply.

But she'd taken the first step. Perhaps peace was achievable.

CHAPTER NINE

Lorne marched in a circuit around the sitting room, the most exercise his ribs and his men would allow.

On the couch, Arne and Godwin were cleaning their daggers and swords, now that their weapons had been returned to them. The others were lounging near the door in deceptively languid positions that belied the fact that they could jump to protect him in a heartbeat if an attack made it past the cordon of Kelvernese guards in the corridor.

Orvyn interlaced his hands behind his head, leaning farther back in the chair where he sat behind the door. "So, Highness, how is wooing your queen going?"

"You shouldn't call me *Highness*." Lorne shot him a glare, hoping the look hid any other emotion that might have strayed across his face.

"Why not? You're a prince consort now. It's your

correct title." Orvyn smirked, ignoring both Lorne's glare and the looks the other guards were sending him.

"A little too correct." Godwin inspected the edge on one of his daggers, deep grooves etched around his mouth.

"It would be more suspicious if we didn't upgrade his title." Orvyn shrugged. "But you didn't answer my question."

"*That* is none of your business." Lorne gritted his teeth, annoyed that the words came out with a growl.

"Ooh. Touchy, touchy." Orvyn smirked wider and wiggled, as if lounging deeper in the chair. "I must be on the right track."

Lorne pressed his mouth shut rather than answering. His march around the room turned into more of a stalk as he pounded his annoyance into the plush rugs.

Emil coughed, adjusting his stance where he leaned against the wall beside the door, his arms crossed. "Begging your pardon, but it is our business. Thanks to certain *things*, peace between Kelverny and Lalsacia is now linked to the harmony between you and your wife. Especially long-term relations between the kingdoms."

Lorne tried not to let his steps falter. Because of his decision to marry Adeline and the fact that they were both the sole heirs of their kingdoms, he'd irrevocably linked Kelverny and Lalsacia. Any disharmony between him and Adeline would be disastrous for both kingdoms.

But he didn't really want to talk about wooing his

wife. In the past week, he'd spent a portion of each day assisting where he could with the various reports and requests that crossed her desk. And he slept beside her every night, becoming increasingly familiar with the soft sounds of her breathing.

He knew such intimate details about her, and yet he knew her so little. She was closed and guarded after years under her grandfather's thumb.

Not that he blamed her. He hadn't been exactly forthcoming with details about himself either, too fearful of slipping up and giving away that he was actually the crown prince of Lalsacia.

That was a truth he wanted to tell her eventually, but the situation in Kelverny was still too precarious for him to burden her with that knowledge just yet.

With a sigh, Lorne spun to face Orvyn. "What are you suggesting?"

"Romantic meal...walk under the stars..." Orvyn ticked off the items on his fingers.

"A meal that could be poisoned. A walk that would make both of us vulnerable." Lorne crossed his arms, then had to adjust the gesture when it pressed on his ribs.

"We'd have to work with the queen's clerk and maid to ensure everything was safe." Orvyn flapped a hand, as if brushing off any concerns. "It's what we've been doing for all of your regular meals."

Lorne dropped his hands back to his sides, relieving the pressure on his ribs. He wasn't sure why he was protesting so much. It wasn't like he was opposed to a romantic dinner and moonlit walk with Adeline. "All right. If you're offering to be my errand boy to arrange it, let's get started."

❧

ADELINE RUBBED AT HER EYES, THE NUMBERS SWIMMING before her. Her head pounded after spending most of the day meeting with the council.

Meeting was far too tame a word for it. Getting yelled at by most of the council was more like it. While the number of lords satisfied with her decisions was growing, and she might even dare to count a few of them as now loyal to her, those who would happily see her fail, if not dethrone her entirely, were still the loud majority.

None of them had, so far, made their move. But they had to be planning something. She could see it in Lord Sarlon's gaze.

A knock sounded on her door a moment before Thaddeus entered. "Your Majesty, it's time for supper."

"Have a tray delivered. I really should finish this." She gestured to the piles of paperwork that never seemed to diminish.

"The paperwork will wait until tomorrow." Thaddeus shook his head and opened the door wider. "Supper awaits in your room."

Considering she could no longer focus on the dancing numbers, she might as well set this aside until tomorrow.

Rising, she rounded the desk, pulling out her key. She locked the door after herself, then swept down the corridor within the protective cordon of her guards and Thaddeus trailing after her.

When she reached her suite, a guard opened the door to her sitting room and stepped aside.

When Adeline strode inside, she halted at the savory smells and intriguing sight that greeted her.

Lord Lorne stood there, wearing finer clothes than she'd seen him in before. The deep blue of the fabric set off the dark browns in his eyes while his dark hair had been neatly combed with just a hint of tousling.

Beside him, a small table was draped in a white lace tablecloth and set for two in fine porcelain dishes. A gold candlestick provided a flickering, warm lighting.

Lorne held out a chair for her. "Supper will be served shortly."

Adeline crept across the room and sank into the chair, entirely unprepared for the way her heart beat harder in her chest. "You arranged all of this?"

"Yes, with a lot of help from Thaddeus, Jelsa, and my men." Lorne took the chair across from her.

As they did for every meal. One of her guards always oversaw the preparation of any food she or Lorne ate. While she was reasonably sure the cook and most of the staff were loyal to her, there was always a risk someone would slip something into her food.

"In the meantime, let's get to know each other." Lorne leaned forward, giving her a smile that held such warmth that Adeline's cheeks flushed with a matching heat. "What's your favorite color? Food? Sunsets or sunrises?"

Adeline clasped her hands in her lap. Those shouldn't be hard questions. But they held meaning, when asked by him. And that made a nervous tumult twist her stomach.

Thanks to her grandfather, she knew the importance of guarding her words. Answering even those mild questions made one vulnerable. It gave the other person ammunition to use against one. A favorite dress color could be forbidden unless she agreed to what he wanted. A favorite food could be withheld or given as a "reward" for manipulated obedience.

His expression softened, and he stretched his hand out to her, resting it on the table between them in an offer without any presumption. "Perhaps you'd rather I went first?"

She managed a nod and, tentatively, reached with one hand to clasp his. The strength in his grip steadied her while knowing he'd speak first eased the nerves.

"To answer my own questions..." Lorne's thumb rubbed over the top of her knuckles. "I can't decide between sunsets and sunrises. They're both beautiful. I love deep purple."

"Lalsacian purple?" Adeline managed a hint of a smile at that.

"What can I say? I love my kingdom." There was a note in his voice, an extra twinkle in his eyes at that.

She smiled in return. He had married her, after all, for the sake of his kingdom. "I'll admit, I'm rather partial to Kelvernese yellow. And…" She couldn't help the way her voice dropped along with her smile. "And pink. I like pink."

She clamped her mouth shut around that admission. She remembered all too well when she'd been fifteen and the maids had come in, ordered by her grandfather to take all her pink clothing. It wasn't a dignified color for a crown princess. She'd been in mourning at the time, not even wearing any color but black.

She'd finally been able to commission the pink dress she wore for her wedding by being particularly obedient to one of her grandfather's demands. Even now that her grandfather was dead, she hesitated at the thought of commissioning another pink dress for herself. Granted, she was stuck in blacks and grays for a while yet, but after that, it still felt like pink would be undignified for a queen.

"Pink is a lovely color." Lorne squeezed her hand, still giving her that soft smile.

Before she could say anything else, the door behind her opened. She glanced over her shoulder, yanking her hand out of Lorne's, as his guard Orvyn and her maid Jelsa entered, each carrying a tray piled with dishes covered with silver domes.

"Would you like us to stay and serve, Your Majesty?" Jelsa bobbed her knees, her hands too full for a true curtsy.

"Or we can set it on the sideboard if you'd rather have privacy." Orvyn shot Lorne a look that held a hint of a smirk. Even in their short acquaintance, it wasn't hard to see that Orvyn was the most prone to teasing and jokes among the diplomatic envoys.

Lorne looked at her, his gaze searching her face, before he gestured to the sideboard. "Put the trays there. I'll serve us."

"Yes, sir." Orvyn somehow managed an elaborate bow before he spun on his heel and placed his laden tray on the buffet beside the door.

Jelsa, too, placed her tray there before the two of them retreated, leaving Adeline alone with Lorne once again.

Lorne stood, peeking under a few of the domes, before he picked up one of the plates, whipped the dome off, and presented the dish to her with a flourish. "Our first course. Leek and potato soup."

Adeline found herself smiling as Lorne placed a bowl of soup before her. Perhaps a romantic dinner making small talk was exactly what she needed.

AFTER A DINNER WHERE SHE FOUND HERSELF TELLING LORNE far more about herself than she meant to, she led him through the corridors until they stepped through a door into a small garden, the outer walls of the castle rising high above them against the starry dark of the night.

A breeze wafted over the walls, carrying with it the scents of the rolling hills that spread out as far as one could see from the castle's windows. The seemingly endless farmland of Kelverny teemed with the herds of cattle and deer and the wild sylon cats that hunted them.

"What was it like, growing up in the dense forests of Lalsacia?" Adeline tipped her face toward the sky, trying to imagine a land where tall trees covered the sky and rain fell so frequently that the sun was rarely seen.

"I never saw so much sky until I visited the mountains the first time." Lorne, too, turned his face upward.

The stars filled the sky in a glittering expanse, vast and unaffected by politics or wars. Lord Sarlon and his ilk could bluster and maneuver as much as they wanted, but no matter how much power they gained, they could never affect the stars.

Dragging her gaze back down, she meandered down her favorite path, the one that wound between peony bushes. At this time of early summer, the buds were just opening, filling the air with a thick, sweet scent.

"Are peonies your favorite flower?" Lorne must have seen something in the way she was lingering.

"Yes." She halted, reached out, and traced a finger over one of the waxy petals.

"Not much of a surprise." He leaned closer, his nearness making her heart pound. "They are your favorite color."

Her cheeks burned, and she couldn't quite meet his gaze. It was too warm, and this moment of sharing such a personal detail made her too vulnerable.

As if sensing her discomfort, Lorne took half a step back to put distance between them and drew in a deep breath, exhaling slowly. "It smells different here. Warmer and sweet somehow. In Lalsacia, it always smells of damp earth and green trees."

She'd love to experience that someday. Would their kingdoms ever be at peace securely enough for her to risk traveling to Lalsacia?

Had she stolen that from Lorne? Would he ever be able to return to that home that he spoke about with such longing, such love?

"One of my favorite things to do is walk through the woods behind my estate first thing in the morning." Lorne's fingers brushed hers, a light touch that asked for permission. "At that time of day, the fleech dragons are waking up, skittering over the trees or flying through the shafts of sunlight. Sometimes I'll spot an elk or a bear. It's peaceful."

Seeing a bear didn't sound so peaceful to her. But then again, she'd grown up riding the hills and watching wild sylon cats stalk their prey, so perhaps that wasn't so dissimilar.

She twined her fingers with Lorne's. "That sounds really nice."

"I hope to show you someday." Lorne swung their clasped hands. When she glanced at him, she found he was already looking at her. His smile softened. "Perhaps that day might be sooner than we think, if we bring about peace between our kingdoms."

"Perhaps." She couldn't bring herself to be as optimistic as he was. Even with peace, there was the problem that she was Kelverny's sole heir. It would be a long time before Kelverny was comfortable with her disappearing into Lalsacia even for a short trip.

But tonight was an evening for letting herself dream, just a little bit.

CHAPTER TEN

Lorne woke, lying there for a long moment as he gathered his senses.

There it came again. The slight scuff of noise that had woken him. A cool breeze whispered across his face, something that shouldn't have been there if the doors to the balcony had been closed.

Lorne cracked his eyes open. He lay with his back to the balcony, and the hair at the back of his neck prickled at being so exposed and vulnerable.

Before him, Adeline slept peacefully, her face toward him and lit by the brightness of the moonlight.

Another scuff, and a shadow fell across Adeline's face. Something glinted.

Lorne wrapped his arms around Adeline and rolled. She woke with a scream as the two of them tumbled off the far side of the bed in a jumble of sheets and limbs.

He took the jolt on his back, groaning as her weight

slammed into his ribs. He coughed as he rolled the two of them again to tuck her against the wall. Another cough, and he managed to drag in enough breath to yell, "Guards! Attack! Guards!"

"What—" Adeline blinked, still bleary and confused.

Lorne shoved himself away, struggling to disentangle himself from the constricting blankets. As he raised his head over the edge of the bed, the dark figure of the assassin lunged, knife flashing.

Grabbing a handful of blanket, Lorne flung it into the assassin's face. The assassin flinched, buying Lorne just enough time to snatch the candlestick from the bedside table. It was small, meant for only a single candle to light the room before bed, but any item in hand was better than nothing.

The door between the bedroom and the sitting room rattled and thumped. The guards shouted, but the door held. The assassin must have taken the time to lock the connecting doors, turning the reassuringly sturdy oak doors into a detriment instead of protection.

Lorne brought the candlestick up. The assassin's knife clanged on it, the blade scraping and screeching as it deflected. Jumping to stand on the bed, the assassin stabbed again, and Lorne dodged as best he could, his feet tangling in the blankets on the floor. With the higher position and far better weapon, the assassin had all the advantages.

Adeline yelped and flung herself out of Lorne's

way. Yet she kept going, racing toward the door as the guards attempted to break it down.

The assassin turned toward her, as if realizing what she was after. Lorne leapt at the assassin, sending him toppling off the far side of the bed. The assassin grunted as he hit the floor, his head and shoulder knocking against the bedside table on that side, sending a book toppling.

Landing stretched out on his stomach on the bed, Lorne scrambled to get to his hands and knees. He'd lost his grip on the candlestick, and it must have gone flying somewhere in the dark. He cast about for something, anything, but the only things near to hand were the pillows. He gripped one, raising it as a pitiful shield.

On the floor, the assassin rolled, the movement taking him several feet from the bed. He hadn't lost hold of his dagger, and another dagger had appeared in his other hand.

Lorne raised the pillow slightly higher. He wasn't liking his chances, bringing a pillow to a knife fight.

The door finally slammed open, accompanied by the stomping of feet, shouts, and the swish of swords.

The assassin took one look at the charging guards and turned to run toward the balcony. Considering they were on the third floor, Lorne wasn't sure the assassin could escape out that way. Unless he could climb as fast as a squirrel or fly like a bat.

As the guards closed in, Lorne hurried to Adeline and drew her into a hug. He held her close as steel clashed, men yelled, and Adeline trembled in his arms.

ADELINE TRIED NOT TO LOOK AT THE BODY ON THE FLOOR, the blood spreading in a dark liquid puddle, as Lorne steered her across her room and toward the connecting door that led to the room designated as his.

The assassin had fought to the end, forcing her guards to kill him. While she was relieved the threat was gone, it also meant they couldn't question him to find out who had hired him.

They paused by the door, waiting, while two of the guards searched the other room. Only once a guard gave them a nod did Lorne lead her inside.

The other room was peaceful and quiet, the bed neatly made. The room was carpeted, upholstered, and draped in deeper, richer colors than her own room while the bed was a heavier, darker walnut.

Lorne steered her toward the bed, then gently lowered the two of them onto it, sitting against the headboard.

Adeline didn't resist, curling against him in the warmth of his arms. She tucked her feet under the covers, not caring about trying to appear dignified.

"Are you all right?" Lorne's voice was soft, his breath whispering against her hair.

"Yes." She wasn't. Not even close. But she was physically all right, so it wasn't a complete lie. "You? That couldn't have felt good on your ribs."

"I'm fine." Lorne's grip tightened around her, as if he heard the truth of how not-fine she was in her voice.

"They're trying to kill me. They're actually trying to kill me." She squeezed her eyes shut as she pressed her face into the hollow of his shoulder. She hadn't realized how it would feel to fit so well against him. Despite his still healing ribs, he had regained a level of strength that she could feel in the arms that held her.

Safe. It had been so long since she'd had someone to hold her tight and safe like this. Not since the last time her father hugged her before her parents left for that ill-fated diplomatic mission to Lalsacia.

"That assassin could have been sent for me, not you." Lorne traced a line down her back, his touch gentle.

"Not exactly comforting." She fisted her hands in the front of the light shirt he'd worn to bed. The assassin hadn't looked particularly picky about which of them he targeted. Had he been ordered to kill Lorne first, then go after her?

Footsteps drew her gaze to the door, where one of the guards had halted. "Your Majesty, we've searched the body. But there's no indication of who hired him."

"Not unexpected." Lorne sighed, shaking his head.

She didn't mind that he answered for her. Not in this moment when all she needed was someone to take over while she clung to him and tried to gather her frayed senses back to a semblance of calm.

When he spoke, Lorne's voice rumbled beneath her ear, his confident tone reverberating through him into her. "He seemed to be somewhat professional. He must have scaled the castle wall to get in, and he took the time to lock the doors before going after us. But he wasn't the most skilled assassin. Otherwise I doubt I could have fought him off."

"That would be our assessment as well." The guard tilted a nod to Lorne.

Adeline worked up enough strength to speak. While she appreciated Lorne stepping in, she had to be the queen and say something, both to assert her authority and to confirm Lorne's in speaking for her up until then. "Thank you for the report."

The guard bowed, nodded, and backed out of the room. He closed the door after him, as if acknowledging it was time to give them privacy while the guards finished cleaning up the mess in the other room.

"You did well in going for the door during the attack." Lorne shifted, and when she glanced up at him, he was smiling down at her. "I'm impressed. I've known a lot of people who would freeze in that situation."

"It was all I could think to do." Adeline gave a shiver, trying not to think too hard about those minutes of waking up to a man swinging a knife at them. "You didn't freeze either. You were pretty heroic, defending us with a candlestick. And a pillow."

"It was desperation more than heroics." Lorne gave a huff of a laugh, but his smile remained.

"I still found it heroic." She smiled up at him, his face only inches from hers. Perhaps it was the fading shock of the assassination attempt, but looking at him stirred something within her. She had the strange urge to erase the distance and press her mouth to his.

His head dipped lower to hers, their breaths hot in the space between them. "Adeline..."

All she could manage was a slight nod. She couldn't even get her tangled tongue to whisper his name.

He closed the last of the distance and kissed her, slowly, gently, a careful exploration rather than pushing her too far, too fast.

She fumbled to kiss him back, the tension melting away into a heat flooding her. It was new and thrilling and as much as she wanted to embrace it, she dreaded it too.

Rather than deepening the kiss, he pulled back a heartbeat later, letting the kiss remain soft and gentle.

"Why did you stop?" She murmured the words, still in a haze.

"There's no reason to rush." He held her just as gently as he'd kissed her.

Perhaps she should have been disappointed, but a relief just as sweet as the kiss filled her instead. She wasn't ready for more. After all, she'd only known Lorne for about a month. Hardly enough time to work up to anything more than a few exploratory kisses.

"It was nice." She rested her head on his shoulder again.

"Only nice?" His light chuckle reverberated in his chest beneath her ear. "That's a blow to my ego."

"I liked nice." Adeline finally let herself relax. Perhaps she might even fall back to sleep.

How was it possible that this man—this enemy lord—could make her feel so safe when she'd never felt this way with any of the other marriage prospects she'd considered?

But Lorne made her dare to hope. Not just for mere safety, but for security for her heart as well.

CHAPTER ELEVEN

Lorne stood in the shadows by the front wall of the council room, his gaze skipping over the various lords assembled in the rows before the dais. Burchard and Godwin stood on either side of him, both poised for trouble.

Who in that room before him sent the assassin? Lorne searched for any sign of guilt. A shift to the feet or a flick of the eyes.

Perhaps he should be looking for someone who appeared too confident. If one of these lords was plotting to kill his queen, he likely didn't feel any guilt about it. He would be convinced he was doing what was best for his kingdom. Or at the very least, what was best for himself.

Adeline sat in her throne-like chair on the dais in front of him as a discussion raged across the room. Something about the taxes needed to support the army, and if food that was destined for the army anyway should be taxed or should be considered the tax on farmers in and of itself.

The ebb and flow of the debate was so familiar that Lorne had to work hard to suppress his smile. He'd sat through many a similar debate among the Lalsacian nobility, although Lalsacia allowed women to inherit noble titles so the council room back home had far more women than the room before him did.

At their heart, Kelverny and Lalsacia weren't all that different. If only they could end this war, perhaps the two kingdoms could figure out a way to be neighbors instead of warring nations.

Once the discussion finally wound down, Adeline stood. After giving a few comments on how she would take their input under advisement, she swept the room with a hard glance.

Lorne had to work to suppress his smile once again. With her back ramrod straight and her expression regal, she was the picture of a queen rather than the trembling, fearful person she'd been the night before after the attack. She would pull this off because she was far stronger than the lords realized.

"As some of you might have heard, last night an assassin broke into my rooms and attempted to kill me and my husband." Adeline's posture didn't shift, her voice didn't waver. "As you can see, we are uninjured. The assassin was apprehended and is being held in the dungeon. My guards expect that he will tell the name of the one who hired him shortly."

Lorne scoured the faces before him once again,

looking for a flicker to betray the man who'd hired the assassin.

While that lord would have known last night that his plan had failed, he would've had no way of knowing whether the assassin had been killed or captured. The guards on duty had been ones loyal to Adeline, and Thaddeus had quickly realized the news of the assassin's death should be kept quiet. They'd come up with this ruse to flush out the lord who orchestrated the assassination attempt.

Lorne couldn't see any betrayal on the faces of the lords before him. There was plenty of shifting and murmuring, and the surprise of finding out their queen had nearly been killed was indistinguishable from the surprise of finding out the assassin had been captured.

Would the lord behind this take the bait? Or would he realize this was a trap?

Likely, he wouldn't go to the dungeon himself to try to kill the assassin. He'd send someone. Probably bribe a guard.

But that guard could be captured and interrogated, and he'd be far easier to break than a semi-professional assassin would have been.

As Adeline turned toward Lorne, her guards closing around her, he stepped forward and held out his arm. He smiled as she took it, her hand light against his sleeve.

He'd originally married her for the sake of peace between their kingdoms. But somewhere along the way, she'd become incredibly precious to him.

And that scared him. What would he be willing to

sacrifice for her sake? If he had to pick between her or Lalsacia, what would he choose?

⁂

Lorne paced in the tiny dungeon cell that had once been his. At least this time, his hands weren't shackled, and his ribs were well on their way to healing. He clutched a sword in his hand, waiting.

Emil, Arne, and several of Adeline's trusted guards waited in the adjoining cells. Since they hadn't announced to the lords exactly which cell the supposedly still alive assassin was being held in, they'd set the trap so that it wouldn't matter which of these cells was opened. They were all poised for an ambush.

Somewhere farther away, a door clanged. Lorne tensed, adjusting his grip on his sword. After the weeks he'd spent in this dungeon, he was intimately familiar with every noise, the way bootsteps echoed in the passages, and the sound of someone halting nearby.

Another door creaked. Not his, but the one next door where Emil was hidden.

"To arms!"

Lorne jumped to his feet and shoved the unlocked door open. The passageway outside was already filling with loyal guards, and he stayed to the side rather than joining the rush.

Another guard was frozen in the doorway of the next cell over, his hand on his sword's hilt. But with several swords already pressed to his chest, he had no chance of running.

"Harry." One of Adeline's guards spat the name. "I should have known you'd be the scum hired for this."

The captured guard sneered back. At that point, sneering was all he could do.

Lorne eased forward, his movement sending the disloyal guard's gaze in his direction. "I'm Lorne, prince consort to Queen Adeline. Things will go easier for you if you tell us who hired you."

"Lalsacian scum." The captured guard spat a glob of spit, which landed on the blade of one of the swords pressed to his chest. He proceeded to lace a few expletives through his insults about Lorne and Lalsacia.

Arne jabbed the traitorous guard slightly harder with his sword. "Insults and swearing won't help you."

The loyal guard who'd spoken before also growled and shoved harder with his sword. "You will tell us one way or another. It's up to you how much you want it to hurt before you do."

Lorne didn't want to order a man tortured the way he and his men had been, but at least this guard would somewhat deserve it for his disloyalty to his queen.

Hopefully it wouldn't come to that. It shouldn't. This man didn't seem like he'd hold up under the threat of torture, much less the real thing.

"It was Lord Fellton." Harry sagged, a desperate edge to his eyes. "He paid me to kill the assassin. He also paid me to let the assassin onto the castle grounds last night."

Lorne tried not to betray his surprise. He'd really thought the guard would say Lord Sarlon, not Lord Fellton. Although, it probably shouldn't surprise him that Lord Fellton hired an assassin who wasn't top-notch and that he'd bribed a guard who would cave under the slightest pressure.

"Thank you for your cooperation." Lorne gave the disloyal guard a hint of a nod. "It will be taken into consideration when the queen names your sentence. In the meantime, enjoy the hospitality of the dungeon."

He stepped aside so that the loyal guards could hustle the disloyal one into a cell, shackling his hands and securely locking the door.

Lorne let the clank of the shutting door sink into his bones. Time to tell Adeline that they'd caught at least one of the threats to her.

ADELINE STARED AT THE REPORT, WHICH DETAILED ALL THE evidence found in Lord Fellton's rooms at the castle and at his estate. There was no question he'd conspired against her and sent that assassin.

Not to mention, she was looking at the proof that the assassin had been sent to kill both her and Lorne.

To think she'd once seriously considered marrying Lord Fellton's son. He'd even been one of her top two picks. What a fortunate thing it had been that she'd made the somewhat rash decision to marry the lord locked in the dungeon instead.

She would have to convene the council again and hold a trial. It would be quite the production with a lord on trial, especially for treason. Nor was she looking forward to having to deliver sentences for both the guard and Lord Fellton.

A knock sounded on the door before Thaddeus stepped inside.

Adeline sighed and tapped the report. "I'm going to have to order his execution, aren't I?"

"Most likely, yes." Thaddeus halted before her desk. "There are limited options for treason, especially conspiring to kill the monarch. You can't be lenient on that. It sets a bad precedent. Banishment might also be an option, but he'd always be out there, even more angry after losing his title and riches."

"I was afraid of that." She really didn't want to have to give such a verdict.

But it seemed being queen involved doing a lot of things she didn't want to do.

When she met Thaddeus's gaze again, she took in the weariness in his eyes. In the weeks since she'd ascended the throne, his hair had gone even more gray, his face more lined. She really ought to find another personal steward. Thaddeus deserved retirement, not the added burdens she placed on him.

Yet there were so few people she trusted, even now. She certainly didn't trust the man who'd been her grandfather's steward, nor any of her grandfather's former staff.

Thaddeus reached into the leather satchel at his side and pulled out a folded and sealed paper. "This arrived by our trusted messenger."

The reply from Lalsacia.

Adeline's stomach twisted, and her hands trembled as she took the paper from Thaddeus. It took her several tries to break the seal. Forcing herself to take a deep breath, she unfolded it and tried to focus enough to take in the words written there in a firm hand. The bottom of the page was signed by King Philip of Lalsacia himself.

"The king of Lalsacia is willing to treat in person." The lift in her chest fell like a stone a moment later. "But he demands the return of the remaining six envoys. Only once we have returned them will he sit down to discuss a peace treaty with me."

"You still haven't told him, have you." Thaddeus spoke the words as a statement, rather than a true question.

She wasn't sure if he was asking if she'd told the king of Lalsacia about her marriage to Lord Lorne or if she'd told Lorne about her negotiations with the king of Lalsacia.

In the end, it didn't matter, as the answer to both of those questions was the same. "No."

Was she making the right choice? And if it was the right choice, then why did her heart hurt so much?

CHAPTER TWELVE

Lorne kept his horse at a walk beside Adeline's as they rode into the mountains that created the border between Kelverny and Lalsacia, surrounded by numerous guards and several Kelvernese lords who filled out the diplomatic party.

Adeline's horse tossed its head, and she flexed her fingers, relaxing her grip on the reins. Still, the tension didn't ease from the line of her back nor the strain from her eyes.

He halted himself before he asked yet again if she was all right. She'd been tense and distant the entire trip from the castle to the mountains, growing more so the closer they came.

Was she merely nervous for the peace talks? A lot hung on the balance. Peace between their kingdoms. Her continued reign. Perhaps her very life.

And yet she was pulling away from him in a way he wouldn't have expected, given that she'd married him with the purpose of peace. Shouldn't she have leaned on him more rather than less? They should have stayed up long into the night, discussing their plans.

Worse, he hadn't yet told her the truth. With so many guards around them in the week and a half since the assassination attempt and with her suddenly holding him at arm's length, he hadn't found the right opportunity.

He would have to tell her soon. Before she came face-to-face with his father and found out then.

They crested a rise, and the sprawling Kelvernese military encampment lay before them, a sea of tents filling the valley all the way up to the rise on the far side. There, a palisade of cut timbers created a wall across the pass. The smallest tents were placed in rows near the barrier with larger tents for the commanders at the rear.

Already, a large tent in Kelvernese dark yellow was rising in a cleared space among the larger tents, Adeline's standard flying from the center pole.

Somewhere out of sight over that rise, Lorne's father would be entering a nearly identical encampment, if he wasn't there already.

Lorne's heart beat harder as it ached within his chest. How he missed his father. Did he know for sure that Lorne was even still alive? Did he know he hadn't been imprisoned the full time he'd been gone? How much had Adeline written in her communications?

Adeline, strangely, hadn't let him see any of the missives sent back and forth. He hadn't even known about them until she'd announced they would be leaving for the border and a diplomatic meeting with the Lalsacian king.

Had he done something wrong? Had that kiss they'd shared scared her away? She'd said it was nice, but she'd withdrawn so soon afterwards.

It was just so...frustrating. He'd thought they were making progress romantically. He'd thought the whole point of their marriage had been for him to assist her in crafting the peace between their kingdoms. Instead he'd found himself shut out as surely as if she'd slammed the door between their bedrooms in his face.

The guards led the way into the encampment, announced with the blaring of trumpets and the march of feet as soldiers assembled into ranks to be presented to their queen.

As Adeline rode between the rows of soldiers, Lorne at her side, the men saluted, all stiff postures and proper uniforms.

Lorne resisted the urge to shudder at the sight of the sylon cats and their handlers. The big cats sat primly, their gray-and-white-striped fur sleek over their lean muscles. When one yawned, it showed off its long teeth.

Adeline halted her horse before the large royal tent. Lorne drew his horse to a halt beside hers and swung down. He reached her side in time to steady her as she climbed down, the heavy skirts of her riding dress swirling around her as she dismounted.

A Kelvernese soldier—the commanding general, based on all the braid and medals on his uniform— approached and bowed low. "Your Majesty. It is a pleasure to welcome you to our humble encampment. We have done all we can to ensure your safety while you are here."

Lorne eased slightly closer to Adeline's back, glancing around. His five guards dismounted and gathered behind him, as her guards did for her.

Farther away, Lord Pellier, Lord Delaney, Lord Harding, and Lord Sarlon, who had insisted on coming, dismounted from their horses with their own retinues surrounding them.

There were so many threats to her. Would Lord Sarlon make a move here? What about another traitor who opposed the thought of peace with Lalsacia?

Then there were his people. How many of them would take the risk of killing the Kelvernese queen, thinking it would lead to peace, when instead they'd end up inciting a far more terrible turn to the war?

"I appreciate your welcome and your care for my security." Adeline gave a tilt of her head to acknowledge the general. "Has the Lalsacian king made contact yet?"

"Yes. He arrived last evening and sent a message." The general made another, smaller bow.

His father was here. Just over that rise. Lorne tried not to look in that direction or otherwise give away his connection to the Lalsacian king. He needed to talk to Adeline. As soon as they finished with the greetings.

"Very good. Please send him a message that I've arrived and that I would like to begin the negotiations as soon as possible." Adeline's tone was that crisp, formal one she used when she was doing her best to be especially queenly. "And…" Adeline's gaze flicked to Lorne for just a heartbeat.

But even that brief look was enough for Lorne to see something aching and tearing in her eyes.

"Adeline?" He reached to touch her hand.

But Adeline took a step out of his reach, her expression and stance never faltering, even as her eyes held heartbreak. "General, please take Lord Lorne and his men into custody."

At her words, the general immediately moved forward, the Kelvernese guards closing in.

"Adeline, please." Lorne held her gaze, even as firm hands settled on his arms, preparing to haul him back. "We need to talk. Please."

Why was she doing this? Surely she knew he wasn't a threat. He'd kissed her, after all. He certainly wasn't going to do anything to sabotage this meeting.

Adeline turned away, her tone somehow unwavering. "Restrain them if necessary, but treat them well. We want them in good shape when we return them to their king."

"Adeline!" Lorne wanted to fight the hands dragging him backward, but it wouldn't do any good, not here surrounded by the whole of the Kelvernese army.

Instead, all he could do was keep his gaze fixed on her retreating back before she disappeared within the royal tent.

"Sir?" Godwin's voice dragged Lorne's gaze to him.

The five of his guards had shifted to stand in a circle, their hands on their swords, although they hadn't drawn their weapons yet. The Kelvernese soldiers faced them, also tensed and poised for action.

"Stand down." Lorne's shoulders slumped as he let the soldiers drag him farther from the tent. "Don't resist."

What was going on with Adeline? Why was she doing this?

Worse, he was too late. He hadn't told her the truth.

"ARE YOU SURE THIS IS THE RIGHT CALL, YOUR MAJESTY?" Thaddeus remained standing near the door of the tent, his hands clasped behind his back. His tone held just the trace of his disapproval, even if his face was impassive. "You married him in order to help you bring about peace."

"I know." Adeline hugged her arms over her stomach as she paced across the tent. "This might make peace harder, but it is what is best for him."

She loved him too much to keep using him. It was time to let him go without the burden of ties to her.

The flap opened, and the general bowed to her. "The Lalsacian king has sent his reply."

"Already?" Adeline spun, her heart pounding harder in her throat. It had only been minutes since they'd arrived and she'd sent off a messenger.

"Yes. He seems quite eager to open the talks." The general straightened. "He requests to meet immediately, if you are amiable."

She wouldn't have the chance to change or clean up after the long ride, but she could forgo those comforts easily enough. Right now, she was so restless that she'd rather just get this over with.

"Yes, I am." Adeline would have straightened her shoulders, but her back already hurt from how straight and correct she was standing. "Send six of our men forward with a tent."

"Very good, Your Majesty." The general bowed before leaving the tent.

Adeline paced while she waited. It took several more back and forths before a tent was set up and furnished, ready for her and the Lalsacian king to meet.

Climbing onto her horse with her crown firmly set on her head, Adeline set out once again, surrounded by her guards and the contingent of lords. She tried not to look over her shoulder toward the rear of the column where Lorne and his men were being marched on foot by a squad of soldiers.

Soldiers opened a door set in the palisade, and then she was riding into the open valley that spread between the two warring armies. On the far saddle-back crest, an identical palisade cut across the land, and a column of riders was coming toward her.

One hundred yards from the tent set in the center of the valley, Adeline halted and dismounted.

Instead of Lorne, it was the general who helped her down from her horse. "I don't like that you will be so alone and vulnerable, Your Majesty."

"The king and I agreed to take only three personal guards each." Adeline wouldn't mention that she would feel safer with only her three most trusted guards at her side. "I will feel more secure with you here where you'll be able to see any larger attack brewing."

She didn't think there would be one. Lorne had hinted how eager the Lalsacian king was for peace. After all, Lalsacia hadn't been the one to start the war. Kelverny had. Lalsacia hadn't killed Adeline's parents. A Kelvernese traitor or her grandfather had. Lalsacia had reached forward the hand of peace first by sending Lorne and his envoys, and it had been Kelverny that had rebuffed the attempts.

Hopefully it wasn't too late for Kelverny to make amends and negotiate peace after all her grandfather had made the kingdom do.

"Our hopes rest on you, Your Majesty." Lord Pellier approached her.

Adeline extended her hand and, when he bowed over it, she found the strength for a small smile. "Thank you for your loyalty, Lord Pellier."

He was one of the few lords who she had trusted enough to witness her wedding to Lorne. Yet he wasn't questioning her, now that Lorne had been relegated back to the status of prisoner instead of entering this meeting at her side as she'd originally envisioned.

"It is my pleasure, Your Majesty." Lord Pellier held his bow for another moment before he straightened and backed away.

Lord Delaney and Lord Harding also bowed over her hand.

Then Lord Sarlon took her hand, squeezing hard

enough that it hurt. "You should not go into this meeting alone, Your Majesty. You should take one of us at your side."

Adeline resisted the urge to yank her hand out of his crushing grip. "The king of Lalsacia is also entering this meeting without his nobles at his side. It is not an insult to my dignity or that of Kelverny."

Nor would she have taken Lord Sarlon with her, regardless of how much he wanted to wield that influence and power.

Lord Sarlon finally let go of her hand, and it took everything in her not to shake out her fingers, glance at them, or otherwise give away how much his tight grip had unsettled her.

Across the way, the Lalsacian king was already making his way toward the tent, only three guards around him as agreed. The rest of his party waited a hundred yards away from the tent, just as hers did.

Adeline motioned for her personal guards. Once they fell in around her, she strode forward, heading across the grassy field toward the Lalsacian king.

As they neared each other, she took him in as best she could without appearing to stare. He had a narrow face, his skin the shade or two darker in tone than the paler Kelvernese. His black hair was threaded with gray at the temples while his crown rested against it with a regal air that she could only hope she somewhat matched.

There was something about him that she couldn't quite put her finger on. It wasn't like she'd ever met him before, and yet he seemed familiar.

The two of them halted beside the tent, facing each other.

King Philip of Lalsacia gave her a bow that consisted more of his head and shoulders than his waist. "Your Majesty."

That was a respectful gesture on his part, acknowledging her first. As the elder royal and the king of the kingdom that had been the most wronged, he'd had every right to stand on his dignity and demand that she bow first.

Adeline gave a returning dip of her head and shoulders, including a slight bob of her knees as well to add an extra level of respect. "Your Majesty."

"Shall we?" The king gestured to the tent.

Adeline nodded and entered the tent first. As she did, a wave of a strange heat flashed over her, a sense almost like dizziness swirling in her head.

Too much stress and anxiety, most likely. She had to get a hold of herself if she was going to keep her head during these peace talks.

Once inside, she found the nearest chair and sank into it, her legs feeling oddly weak. She didn't care if the Lalsacian king thought it offensive that she hadn't stood on ceremony.

King Philip ducked to enter the tent, glanced around, and sat in a chair on the other side of the tent, leaving plenty of space between the two of them.

One of her guards and one of his entered the tent, but the rest remained outside.

King Philip eyed her, the lines around his mouth giving him an even more grim look. Yet his eyes held an almost painful desperation that she didn't think he realized she could see. "I will not open these negotiations until my envoys are returned."

"Of course." That had been his one stipulation. Adeline motioned to her guard. "Please have the Lalsacian envoys brought here."

"Very well." The guard stepped to the tent flap and passed the message along to her other guards without fully leaving the tent or letting her out of his sight.

Once he'd done that, he returned to his place, and a heavy silence fell over them. Apparently the Lalsacian king wouldn't say so much as a word to her until the envoys were returned.

That was just as well. The longer they sat there, the more Adeline's head swirled and her stomach churned. She was growing flushed, the tent feeling like it was baking in the sun. Would it be too much to ask that the tent flap be opened to let in a breeze to cool off the sweltering, stale air here? She hadn't thought the summer weather would be this oppressive in the mountains.

The Lalsacian king, too, appeared uncomfortable. He stared at the tent flap, one of his knees bouncing slightly, his fingers tapping on his leg. She didn't think he even realized he was giving away his tension with those restless gestures.

Many long, tense minutes later, the tent flap opened, and one of her soldiers stepped inside.

King Philip stilled, his entire being riveted on the tent door in a way that didn't fully make sense. She understood a king being concerned for diplomatic envoys, whom he'd sent into a bad situation. But this level of worry seemed beyond the norm.

Not that she had a lot of energy to process the king's reactions. Her head was going a bit fuzzy, and she had to blink several times to clear her vision.

Emil strode inside first and bowed to his king. As he straightened, he met the king's gaze with a speaking look before he stepped to the side to give more room.

Arne, Burchard, Godwin, and Orvyn followed, each of them bowing to their king before walking deeper into the tent. None of them were bound or gagged, so they must not have resisted as much as she feared they would.

Then Lorne stepped into the tent, his gaze snapping to her with a searing look that froze her breath in her chest.

The Lalsacian king was on his feet as soon as the flap closed behind Lorne. He rushed forward and enfolded Lorne in an embrace, his voice choked. "Lorne."

"Father." Lorne hugged the king in return, his gaze slipping away from Adeline to focus on the man before him.

Adeline's head grew even more light.

Father. Lorne had just called the Lalsacian king *father.*

What had she done. She hadn't married a mere lord. She'd married a Lalsacian prince. *The* Lalsacian prince.

Lorne exchanged a few murmurs with his father,

the words too low for her to make out past the buzzing in her ears. Then Lorne was pulling away from his father's embrace and stalking across the tent toward her, something in his gaze intent.

He braced his hands on the armrests on either side of her, pinning her in her seat without so much as touching her. His face was nearly level with hers as he bent over her. "Just what were you thinking back there?"

"I...I..." Between the buzzing from the revelation of his true identity and the gumminess filling her mouth, she struggled to get her tongue to form words. "My kingdom stole you from your home. I couldn't steal your future. I had to let you go. You couldn't have returned home free of Kelverny if you'd ridden into this meeting at my side. You didn't have a choice in that dungeon, so I wanted to give you a choice now."

"What were you expecting? That I would just ride away into Lalsacia without a backward glance, glad to have my freedom?" Lorne's eyes burned into hers. "I married you. And I take my wedding vows very seriously."

"Married!" King Philip gasped the word from somewhere behind Lorne.

"Such things can be ended. Especially if... because..." She couldn't manage to get the words out, her whole body flushing hotter.

Lorne lifted one hand to grasp her chin, the gesture firmer than a mere cradling yet still somehow gentle as he continued to hold her gaze. "I made my choice, Adeline. My choice is you."

She should have been cherishing those words. Maybe even pushed herself out of the chair and flung herself into his arms.

But a wave of heated dizziness crashed over her, stealing the strength from her limbs and catching her breath in her chest in a way that made her struggle to breathe.

Lorne's gaze narrowed, and his brow furrowed. He shifted his hand from her chin to press his palm to her forehead. "You're burning up. Are you feeling all right? Adeline?"

"I...I think I've been poisoned." It was the only explanation for how suddenly this sickness had come on. She'd felt fine all day.

Her limbs shook with a sudden, cold tremor that crashed hard on the heels of the flashing heat.

After all their precautions, all their diligence, she was going to die just like her parents had. Killed by a traitor from her own kingdom.

CHAPTER THIRTEEN

The jolt of fear washed away whatever exasperated fury Lorne had been nursing. What did his annoyance with her—made more fondness than true anger after hearing her explanation—matter when she was dying?

Lorne gathered Adeline up in his arms. She was shivering, as if caught in a snowstorm, and he cradled her close against his chest. "You're going to be all right."

She tucked her head against his shoulder, her grip tightening.

He turned, shooting a look at his father. "She needs the fleech dragons."

His father nodded as he hurried to open the tent flap, holding it open as Lorne ducked through, Adeline in his arms.

"I'll fetch a horse." Orvyn burst out of the tent on Lorne's heels.

"The queen! The queen has been poisoned!"

The shout came from the group of Kelvernese lords and guards who had come with Adeline and stopped a hundred yards away.

Lorne spun to face that direction, even as several of the lords and guards sprinted toward the tent. Behind him, there came a shout of "Protect the king!" from the Lalsacian guards.

This war could spark all over again at any moment.

Likely the intent of the lord who had poisoned Adeline. Lord Sarlon was lingering back, strolling forward but not joining the surge to protect his queen. After all, he wouldn't want to die in the battle he was in the process of starting.

Adeline wiggled in Lorne's grip, a clear sign that she wanted to stand. He set her down, and she took a tottering step away from him, somehow straightening her shoulders. She lifted a hand, her voice rising to carry over the hubbub. "Halt, everyone! No one is attacking anyone."

Her voice sliced with enough conviction, enough command, that the Kelvernese guards and lords staggered to a halt only a few yards away. When Lorne risked a glance over his shoulder, the Lalsacian guards had halted as well, although they had pulled his father into their midst.

That left Adeline and Lorne alone. Just two people standing in the gap, trying to prevent the war from resuming right then and there.

"Lord Sarlon." Despite the shivering he could see

still quivering her body, Adeline's voice remained strong. "How did you know I was poisoned?"

Farther up the hill, Lord Sarlon crossed his arms, a slight shift to his feet giving away that he felt anything but calm. "You are clearly unwell."

"Am I? And you could tell that from way over there?" Adeline waved her hand. Then her gaze dropped to her hand, her eyes widening. "It was your ring, wasn't it? There's a mark from when you gripped my hand. You poisoned me."

The Kelvernese guards and other lords were glancing between Adeline and Lord Sarlon, something almost like dawning comprehension crossing their faces.

Lorne stepped slightly closer to Adeline. How much longer would she stay standing? Everything in him wanted to sweep her back into her arms and spirit her away to Lalsacia where the fleech dragons could heal her.

But if he did that, war would break out. There was no telling how Lord Sarlon and his cronies would spin the Lalsacian crown prince abducting their queen.

"Did you kill my parents? Or was that my grandfather's doing?" Adeline's gaze remained fixed on Lord Sarlon.

If Lorne hadn't been looking at Lord Sarlon, he wouldn't have seen the start, the way the lord's eyes swung away just for a moment.

Lord Sarlon had been involved in killing Adeline's parents. He'd helped in starting this whole war in the first place, and he was trying to kill Adeline and prolong it now.

Gently resting his hand on Adeline's lower back, Lorne faced the Kelvernese. "Lalsacia didn't kill Crown Prince Elric and Princess Delia. We never wanted this war. But someone in Kelverny did."

All eyes were focused on Lord Sarlon. He took a step back, his hand dropping to the sword at his waist.

"Guards, arrest Lord Sarlon for treason against the crown." Adeline pointed, the gesture still strong despite the tremble he could see in her.

The guards rushed Lord Sarlon. He turned to flee, but he had nowhere to go. The guards quickly tackled him, flattening him to the ground.

"Be careful of the poison!" Adeline shouted, but Lorne wasn't sure anyone could hear her over the commotion of the arrest. Her knees buckled, and Lorne caught her before she fell.

Thaddeus appeared out of the crowd. "They'll search him. Surely he'll have the antidote on him. He wouldn't want to accidentally poison himself."

"If he were smart, he'd have taken the antidote already and no longer has it on him." Lorne swept Adeline into his arms again. She was shaking even harder, curling in on herself as if her stomach hurt. "Nor would I trust anything from Lord Sarlon's hands. Any supposed antidote he provided might just be even more poison."

The lines in Thaddeus's face deepened. "Then..."

"I'm taking her to Lalsacia." Lorne spun and marched toward the Lalsacian lines. Thaddeus and the

Kelvernese lords would have to finish calming things down. He didn't dare wait any longer.

Orvyn hurried forward, tugging a large black horse and a large chestnut on leads in each hand. "Sir."

Just a hint of a smile creased Lorne's face as he took in the black horse. Warrior, his own destrier. His father must have brought the horse along in anticipation of Lorne's return.

Lorne had to pass Adeline to Orvyn to swing into the saddle. Once Orvyn handed her back, Lorne settled her in his lap as best he could. The high pommel of the saddle must have been digging into her hip, but she didn't complain as she held onto him, her face pressed into his shirt.

With one arm around her to hold her steady, Lorne gripped the reins and nudged Warrior with a squeeze of his legs and a click of his tongue.

Warrior burst into a trot, then smoothed into a canter. The Lalsacian guards parted, giving him a clear path. As he plunged onto the other side, Godwin and Orvyn rode into place beside him. If any of Adeline's Kelvernese guards managed to grab horses and join them, Lorne didn't look back to find out.

He cantered up the hill toward the wooden palisade cutting across the landscape. As they neared, Godwin began shouting, ordering the soldiers there to open the gates in the name of the prince.

The gates swung open, and Lorne's destrier charged through without slowing his pace. On the other side, soldiers hurried out of their way as Lorne led the charge through the Lalsacian encampment, its layout nearly identical to what he'd seen on the Kelvernese side.

Then he was out on the far side, his horse charging down the slope of the saddleback ridge.

He kept the destrier at a steady canter for some time, keeping an eye on the horse's gait and feeling his steady breaths between his legs. As much as Lorne wished to push the horse, pushing the destrier too hard wouldn't help Adeline.

As a war horse, the destrier was bred for carrying the heavy weight of an armored soldier and its own armor into battle. Unlike a saddle horse, the destrier held up under the weight of two people far better, as it wasn't that much different than a man in heavy gear.

After a while, he let the horse slow into the walk, the destrier's nostrils flared and his chest heaving but no more than he would have in a charge into battle.

In Lorne's arms, Adeline convulsed, then turned her head to retch. He adjusted his grip on her to let her heave and retch to one side of the horse. Transferring the reins to the hand around her waist, he smoothed her hair away from her face.

There was nothing more he could do but hold her and get her to the fleech dragons as quickly as possible.

Once the destrier had rested, he nudged it back into that easy canter, despite the desperation shuddering through him to kick the horse into a gallop.

He wasn't sure how many miles passed as he, Godwin, and Orvyn alternated walking and cantering the horses. Around them, the mountains grew more forested, the foothills more rolling.

In his arms, Adeline went from retching and shivering to lying still, and the only things letting him know she was still alive were the faint breaths on his cheek and her occasional shudder in his arms.

The road ahead darkened as it disappeared into the thick vastness of the Donnaris Forest. Dense stands of spruces, cedars, and pines intermingled with a handful of oaks and maples that had somehow managed to grow between the evergreens.

Once they were fully enclosed by the trees, Lorne drew Warrior to a halt. The destrier didn't prance or toss his head at having to stop as he normally would. Instead, he stood there, blowing and lathered, as done in as Lorne had ever seen the large horse.

Without waiting for the others to dismount, Lorne swung his leg over the saddle and slid to the ground with Adeline in his arms. His knees nearly buckled, and he had to stagger several steps to regain his balance. But he didn't fall, and he didn't drop Adeline.

He strode away from the horse, trusting that one of his men would see to walking Warrior to cool him off. Instead, he tottered a few yards deeper into the forest before he sank to a mossy spot at the base of a cedar, Adeline still clutched in his arms. Her head lolled against his arm, her face so achingly pale that he pressed trembling fingers to her throat to check that her heart was still beating.

Her pulse was there, thready and faint. She wouldn't linger much longer.

Lorne gathered a deep breath and let out an undulating, chittering call.

For long moments, nothing happened. The birds and squirrels fell silent. Only the whisper of a breeze in the needles overhead broke the quiet. Even the crunch of the horses' hooves as his men led them in circles seemed muted in the stillness of the forest.

Lorne let out another chittering call. Were there any fleech dragons in the vicinity? Were they close enough to hear him?

While the occasional fleech dragon bonded with a human and became more or less domesticated, the majority of the fleech dragons remained bonded only to the land, wild and yet responding when called upon by anyone in Lalsacia to heal.

He waited several more breathless seconds, mentally tracking Adeline's heartbeats to ensure that she was still alive.

There came a skittering in the tree overhead, sounding somewhat like a squirrel yet with an extra scraping of scales and claws. An answering chitter called from above before a yellow-green fleech dragon scurried into view. It was about the size of a weasel with a similarly long and sinewy body. Scales, larger than that of a snake or typical lizard, covered the dragon while sawtooth ridges ran down its back from the top of its head to the tip of its tail. Tiny wings were folded against its back.

A few yards from the ground, it unfurled its wings, pushed away from the tree, and glided the last few feet to the ground, landing lightly on the moss next to Lorne and Adeline.

Lorne laid Adeline on the moss, his gaze fixed on the fleech dragon. "Please. Help her."

The fleech dragon scurried closer, its body wiggling and waddling. It sniffed at Adeline's face, its tiny nostrils flaring as its slitted, golden eyes squinted.

It lifted its head and let out a louder, screeching call.

All around the forest, other screeching chitters answered before more claws skittered on bark and loam. Fleech dragons in jewel colors from bright red to cerulean blue appeared, bounding over the forest floor or gliding between the huge trunks of the trees.

The first fleech dragon crawled onto Adeline's chest and curled up there like a cat preparing to snooze in the sun. It began making a growling, purring noise deep in its chest. That sound seemed to reverberate outward until Lorne could feel it in his chest as much as hear it with his ears.

As more of the fleech dragons arrived, curling up on or next to Adeline, they also rumbled their purr. A golden glow pulsed, so faint at first that it almost seemed a trick of the light. As it strengthened, little star-bursts drifted around the fleech dragons and Adeline.

Lorne held his breath and Adeline's hand. Would this work? Fleech dragons couldn't heal everything. Lorne's mother would still be alive if that were the case.

He couldn't lose her. Not like this. Not after every-thing. He'd begun to lose his heart to her, and he could see himself falling utterly and completely, if he hadn't already. He wanted to hold her as they celebrated their first child. Their second. The many years of a long and happy marriage.

He'd done all he could for her. All he could do now was sit there, his gaze fixed on the fleech dragons, and hope the magic of those tiny dragons was enough to save her.

CHAPTER FOURTEEN

Awareness came slowly. It started with the sense of warmth and comfort. Then a settling into her own body, her heartbeat strangely loud, her breaths whooshing in and out.

There was something warm behind her, and something equally warm and also heavy on her chest.

Peeling her eyes open, Adeline blinked as she tried to focus. She seemed to be in a forest unlike anything she'd ever seen, denser and darker with larger trees than any found in Kelverny. Sunlight slanted through the huge tree trunks, dust motes shimmering.

A creature lay curled on her chest. Something yellow-green and scaled with tiny wings and a cute little snout that was puffing hot breath toward her face.

Was that one of the fleech dragons she'd heard so much about? It was even smaller—and cuter—than she'd realized.

As she turned her head to take in more of her

surroundings, she became aware of how her head rested against a shoulder, her back against a solid chest. Strong arms braced her up and held her close.

"Adeline?" Lorne's voice spoke near her ear as he gently brushed her hair from her face. "How are you feeling?"

"Alive." She tried to assess the sensations throughout her body. There was no pain, a sweet relief after the tearing she'd felt in her last moments of consciousness. Instead, her whole body felt so relaxed she wasn't sure she could bring herself to move. "I'm all right, I think. I'm just too tired to move."

"Nearly dying is exhausting." Lorne pressed a light kiss to her hair, his arms tightening around her briefly. "Are you up for moving? There's a village about an hour away where we can spend the night."

Adeline nodded and struggled to sit up. It wasn't an easy feat, given how weak her muscles felt and the small dragon sleeping on her chest.

At her movements, the dragon gave a grumbling, chirping sound and lifted its head. It languidly rolled into her lap as Lorne helped her sit all the way upright. She gathered the dragon into her arms as Lorne picked her up, an arm under her knees and the other across her back.

She ran her fingers down the dragon's sleek scales. "I think this one is coming with us."

Lorne smiled down at her, then at the fleech dragon. "Yes. It might still return to the forest. Most fleech dragons prefer to live in the wild. But sometimes they bond with a person."

"Really?" Adeline ran a hand over the fleech dragon's scaly back as Lorne carried her between the huge trees toward where Godwin and Orvyn waited by three horses.

She felt like a package as she was passed first to Orvyn while Lorne swung onto the black destrier, then handed up to Lorne. He settled her on his lap again, her hip pressing against the pommel in a way that was mildly uncomfortable. But with how shaky her arms were and the fleech dragon curled against her, she didn't think she would have been able to hang on to Lorne's waist if she'd sat behind him.

Once the guards settled on their horses, Godwin led the way down the road with Orvyn taking up the rear, placing Lorne and Adeline between them. This time, they rode at a walk, sparing the horses, which had already been pushed hard that day.

The steady rhythm of the horse's gait and the faint grumbling purr of the fleech dragon in her arms threatened to lull her to sleep again. Adeline rested her head on Lorne's shoulder, closing her eyes, so very tempted to give in to the pull.

But under the soothing clop of the horses' hooves on the dirt road, her mind churned through everything.

Lord Sarlon's grip on her hand that had disguised the prick of his poisoned ring.

Nearly dying.

Lorne's true identity.

She very much didn't want to think about the first two. That left addressing the last. Gathering her courage and a deep breath, she forced out the words. "You're the crown prince of Lalsacia. Lalsacia's only heir."

"Yes." Lorne's arms tightened around her. But when she cracked her eyes open and tipped her head enough to peer up at him, his gaze remained focused on the road ahead. Almost fixedly so, as if he couldn't bring himself to look at her.

"Are we actually married?" Her chest went tight at the question. In her arms, the fleech dragon stirred, raising its head and blinking at her as if it had been awakened by her tension.

"Yes. While I didn't use my full name, I used enough of it to be legal." Lorne still didn't look at her. "I signed my full name, but no one bothered to pay too much attention to the length of the scribble. Since my father is Philip, I go by Lorne with those close to me."

She shouldn't have felt this twisting relief in her chest. After all, she had just tried to sever their marriage by giving him the chance to walk away and pretend it never happened. And it would have been far simpler for their kingdoms if they weren't legally married.

"But...why?" She'd had no idea what she'd done the moment she married him. But he'd known exactly what he was doing and all the ramifications of the sole heir to Lalsacia marrying the only heir to Kelverny. "Why marry me, knowing we are who we are?"

"Because I wanted peace between our kingdoms, and this was the only path I saw to get it." After a long moment, Lorne finally tipped his head down to face her, his dark brown eyes searching her face. "And I saw a princess barely clinging to her composure, so desperate that she was proposing marriage to a stranger in her dungeon. I wanted to help her. I couldn't let her keep fighting her battles alone."

"Lorne..." She disentangled one of her arms to wrap it around him as she pressed her lips to his.

Dropping the reins, he gathered her up in both arms as he kissed her in return. The horse continued steadily walking forward, following the horse ahead of it. The fleech dragon in her lap gave another grumble and huff. And Orvyn behind them was surely witnessing every moment.

And yet Adeline didn't care. She found she didn't even care all that much about her remaining questions, pressing as they were. All she wanted to do was melt into his arms.

But after a moment, he pulled back, his gaze still focused on her face. "I wanted to tell you. At first, I didn't dare. Then I wasn't sure how to confess my true identity. I thought I'd have more time, but you negotiated with my father behind my back. I had been about to tell you when you had me sequestered with the guards."

Right. He hadn't been the only one keeping secrets. Things probably would have been far simpler if she had let him write a letter to the Lalsacian king. She'd resisted, wanting to control what the king knew. By doing so, she'd only heightened the king's worry for his son and prevented Lorne from reassuring his father that he was all right.

A chill speared through her. Had she been acting just like her grandfather? By keeping Lorne in the dark and manipulating the situation to control those involved. While control and manipulation were all she had known for five years, she couldn't let herself fall into those same patterns the moment she held authority.

"I'm sorry. I truly did want to offer you a way to return to your kingdom if you wished. I wanted to set you free." Adeline fisted her hand in the back of his shirt. Did he still feel trapped, despite his protestations? As the sole heir of Lalsacia, his true duty lay there, not with her.

"Adeline." Lorne gave a shake of his head, a fond smile on his face. "I choose you. I chose you all the way back there in the dungeon. While I appreciate what you were trying to do—and I understand why offering me the choice of freedom was so important to you—I'm not going anywhere."

He kissed her again, another sweet and slow kiss that didn't press for more.

A loud cough came from behind them. "Sir, perhaps it would be best to refrain from engaging in, uh, such things until we have you safely ensconced in a room at the inn."

Lorne pulled back and gave Adeline a lopsided smile before he glared over his shoulder at Orvyn. "I thought you were all for this developing into a romance."

"Yes, but not where I have to witness it." Orvyn scowled in fake annoyance that would have had her grandfather ordering him thrown back into the dungeon had he seen that look on one of his guards.

"Fine." Lorne picked up the reins once again, facing forward.

Adeline settled her head on his shoulder once again, closing her eyes. She let herself be lulled into a light doze by the soothing rhythm of the horse and the warmth of Lorne and the fleech dragon.

After what must have been an hour, although Adeline couldn't have said for certain, Lorne gave her a slight shake. "We're here."

She blinked her eyes open, finding herself still in his arms on his horse. But instead of the thick forest around them, they were now riding down the street of a small village. Instead of the wood and thatched roofed homes seen in Kelverny, these buildings were mostly built of stone with clay tiled roofs. Smoke drifted from the various chimneys, filling the air with the scent of burning wood.

The people on the streets paused to gape at them. Did they recognize their prince? Or merely recognize that only nobility of some type would be riding destriers this fine?

Adeline straightened, then reached to pat at her hair. She must be a bedraggled sight after the hours she'd spent on a horse in the past few hours. Had it only been that day that she'd arrived at the Kelvernese camp? It felt like far longer.

At the far end of the street, the largest building was the two-story stone inn with clay tiles on the roof just like the rest of the buildings around it. Before the building, several stablehands were in the process of untying a series of destriers and leading them around the building toward the stable. Several soldiers stood in front of the inn doors, an extra purple sash across the fronts of their uniforms.

Lorne halted his horse. Once the guards halted and dismounted, Orvyn approached them and helped Adeline down. Her knees buckled as soon as her feet touched the ground, and with her arms full of fleech dragon, she would have fallen over if Orvyn hadn't gripped her elbow to steady her.

Lorne jumped down moments later, moving as if to pick her up again.

Adeline shook her head, taking a staggering step away from him. "I can walk."

"All right." Instead of picking her up, Lorne wrapped a steadying arm around her waist, keeping her upright as the two of them walked toward the inn.

At the door, the Lalsacian guards both bowed before one spoke. "Your Highness, His Majesty arrived a few minutes ago."

"Thank you." Lorne nodded to them.

Adeline's stomach twisted, although it wasn't from the poison this time. "Your father's here? How did he know to come?"

"He would have guessed we'd come here after you were healed. It's the closest village." Lorne waited another moment for the soldiers to open the doors before he steered her inside. "He must not have wanted to wait to talk until we returned to the front tomorrow."

Understandable, she supposed. The man had spent months worrying about his son in the hands of the enemy, only to have mere minutes to see that he was all right before Lorne had to rush off to save her.

Then there was the whole marriage thing. He was sure to have questions about that.

A servant directed them up the stairs toward the largest parlor the inn had.

Adeline's legs went so shaky again that she could barely climb the stairs, even with Lorne's steadying grip at her elbow. She clutched the fleech dragon to her chest, thankful the creature hadn't left her just yet. She would have been far more of a mess without the soothing purring coming from the little thing.

But here in Lalsacia, she needed to walk with her head high, standing as tall as she could as the queen of Kelverny.

Another pair of guards stood before the door at the top of the stairs. With a bow, one of them opened the door and stepped aside.

With a glance at her, Lorne led the way inside, although he returned his hand to lightly rest on her back once she stepped in after him.

The Lalsacian king sprang to his feet, the deep worry lines etched into his face much as they had been in those moments he'd been waiting in the tent with her before Lorne had been brought in.

The king hurried across the room, but he halted short of them this time, his gaze flicking between them and the fleech dragon she still held. The set of his shoulders eased, although his hands remained poised at his sides as if he wasn't quite sure what to do with them.

"Father, I'd like to officially introduce you to my wife, Queen Adeline of Kelverny." Lorne's hand on her back was just as warm and steady as his voice. His smile was wide as he looked from his father down at her. "I love her."

Adeline started, gaping up at Lorne. He hadn't said those words to her, and yet he was stating them so boldly to his father.

King Philip was gaping too, but he gathered himself after a moment, snapping his mouth shut. When he smiled, the expression held a hint of polite strain. "Welcome to the family, Your Majesty."

"Adeline." She worked to plaster her own strained smile on her face. "Call me Adeline. We are family."

Family. With the Lalsacian king. She couldn't quite comprehend it.

But the word seemed to relax the set of King Philip's shoulders. His smile lost some of the strain, and in the genuineness of it she saw the resemblance between Lorne and his father all the more strongly. "And you can call me Philip. Or Father, if you'd like. It seems I'm now your father-in-law."

He opened his arms. It took her far too long to recognize the gesture as the offer of a hug.

Her eyes filling, she stepped into the embrace. She hadn't been hugged by a father figure in five years. Not since her own father had hugged her farewell before that mission that had led to her parents' deaths. Her grandfather certainly hadn't hugged her.

The Lalsacian king embraced her gently, holding her for only a moment before letting go.

When she stepped back, Lorne wrapped his arm around her shoulders, pulling her close, as if he sensed her need for steadiness in that moment.

King Philip glanced between the two of them. "I see both of you are done in. Let's all get some sleep. I'll send a messenger back to the front to alert the Kelvernese that their queen is well. Hopefully they'll trust my word enough for that. In the morning, we can reconvene and hash out both a peace treaty and some of the complications caused by your marriage."

Adeline nodded and leaned more heavily against Lorne. She was more than ready for sleep. They could deal with politics in the morning.

CHAPTER FIFTEEN

When Lorne woke, Adeline was still deeply asleep beside him with the fleech dragon curled up on her other side, still giving that little rumbling purr even in sleep.

Reaching over, Lorne brushed a strand of her hair from her face, his touch so light that she didn't even stir.

He'd come so close to losing her. A part of him—a large part—wanted to whisk her away to the heart of Lalsacia where she would be safe and happy. Hang the consequences of war and political fallout for Kelverny if their queen never returned.

She'd never agree to it. As much as her grandfather tried to break her, she had a determination he'd never been able to steal. No matter how hard it was, she'd rule Kelverny with a hand that, while not the oppressive one of her grandfather, would still be strong and courageous.

As her prince consort, he would be there at her

side, supporting her every step of the way. And on a day in what he hoped was a future a long, long time off, she would stand at his side as his queen consort when he became the king of Lalsacia.

After easing out of the bed and dressing, Lorne made his way out of the room he and Adeline had been given and down the hall to the sitting room where they'd met with his father the night before. The rumble of talking echoed up the stairs from the taproom below, and he thought he caught a few Kelvernese accented voices in the hubbub. Likely some of the Kelvernese guards had arrived during the night after receiving his father's note.

Once he stepped inside, he found his father already there, perusing a few messages while he ate his breakfast. A tray with a few covered dishes waited on a side table for other early risers.

"Good morn—" Lorne began, but his father was on his feet, crossing the room, and pulling Lorne into a crushing hug before Lorne even managed to get the full greeting out. Lorne *oof*ed out a breath and returned the hug, just with somewhat less force than his father. "I'm all right. Nothing happened to me overnight."

"Indulge me another moment." His father's grip didn't loosen. "I spent weeks not knowing what was happening to you or if you were even still alive."

"I'm sorry I wasn't able to get word to you sooner." Lorne patted his father's back. He'd known those months had to have been hard on his father. After losing Lorne's mother, all they had were each other. "I didn't want to give away who I was, so I had to be careful how I asked for information and how much I pushed.”

“No, you were wise in that. Especially with things so unsettled in the Kelverny court and between our kingdoms.” His father finally released him, but he didn’t take a step back. His gaze searched Lorne’s face. “I spoke with Godwin. He told me about...what happened in the dungeon.”

Lorne didn’t miss the hesitation, as if his father couldn’t bring himself to say *torture* out loud when it came to his son.

An irrational irritation stirred in his chest. He had hoped to keep the full truth of what had happened to him from his father. Surely there had been no reason to burden his father like that. It was over and done. And with Adeline on the throne, it wouldn’t happen again.

But of course, Godwin wouldn’t prevaricate when confronted by his king. He might have even felt compelled to relay the whole of it since he’d known that Lorne wouldn’t.

Lorne sighed, glancing away. “I’m fine. It was hard.” He’d come so very close to breaking, down there in the dungeon. He’d been one torture session away from collapsing into a sobbing, begging mess. “But then Adeline came, and...well, she saved me. I married her out of sheer desperation at first, but then she became so much more to me.”

“You’ve grown.” His father’s gaze still searched his face, but his expression held a smile, a note of pride in his voice.

Lorne nodded. His father didn’t just mean that he’d

toughened after experiencing a harsher reality than anything he'd known before. But it was more than that. He was more able to face the harder things with compassion and gentleness. He'd left a brash boy filled with the overconfidence that he could end this war, and he'd returned a man prepared to give of himself in a way he hadn't been before. "I have."

Father nodded and took a step back. "I look forward to getting to know your wife better."

"You'll like her. She's nothing like her grandfather." Lorne flexed his fingers at his sides. "She needs family in her life. I might have suffered for a few weeks under her grandfather, but she suffered for years. It's telling that the fleech dragon is bonding with her, not me."

There were many theories on why some fleech dragons bonded with a person. But most often, the bonding occurred with a person who needed healing in some way.

While Adeline had been physically healed, she would battle the effects of her grandfather's manipulation and degradation for the rest of her life. That wasn't something that would go away quickly, even with a fleech dragon's soothing magic.

"I will do my best." His father turned and strolled back to his seat. "I will gladly provide any support or mentoring she wishes as a new monarch, but it will be tricky. Kelverny will not be comfortable with the Lalsacian king having too much influence over their queen."

"They'll have to get used to it, considering their prince consort also happens to be the heir to the Lalsacian throne." Lorne shrugged as he headed for the side table. After grabbing an empty plate, he lifted the covers on the dishes and helped himself to the sausages, eggs, and toast provided. The savory scents of the breakfast set his stomach to rumbling.

"A problem we'll need to discuss during the official diplomatic meeting." His father sat, picked up a mug, and took a sip of his coffee. "While it was a rather brilliant move on your part, marrying the Kelvernese queen, it does leave us in a rather interesting political pickle."

"Yes." Lorne re-covered the dishes, crossed the room, and took the seat across from his father. "But I don't regret it."

There was a reason heirs to thrones—especially sole heirs—didn't marry each other, leaving that duty to younger siblings or daughters of high-ranking nobles. Kingdoms didn't just merge because their royalty had done so, and Kelverny and Lalsacia weren't even starting from a position of peace but from the bitterness of five years of war.

But once they had his father, Adeline, Thaddeus, and Lorne all in the same room, he trusted that they'd figure something out.

CLUTCHING THE FLEECH DRAGON TO HER CHEST—THE dragon didn't seem to want to leave her side, much less her arms—Adeline made her way from the bedroom toward the parlor she vaguely recalled from the night before.

When she'd woken, she'd discovered Lorne gone, and a bag with some of her things left beside the bed. She'd felt a lot more herself after washing up with the water and basin, and she was thankful she could change into a clean dress instead of having to put on the dress from the previous day. That dress was currently missing. Presumably the inn staff was attempting to clean it of her vomit, sweat, and dirt from the forest floor from the day before.

She shuddered to remember how she'd hugged the king of Lalsacia while wearing that rather soiled garment.

Worse, she'd kissed Lorne before having the chance to brush her teeth.

As she opened the door to the parlor, she was hit with the sound of laughter and multiple voices.

Inside, the king of Lalsacia, Lorne, and Thaddeus sat in a circle, empty plates on the tables showing they'd already eaten breakfast. They were all smiling—Lorne seemed to have been laughing a moment ago—and even Thaddeus had a smile, even if his posture remained stiff and professional in the presence of a king and prince.

"Adeline." Lorne spotted her first, hopping to his feet and hurrying toward her.

Behind him, Thaddeus stood and bowed, sheer relief in every line of his face and the easing of his posture. "Your Majesty. It is good to see you awake and well."

"I'm sorry to have worried you." Adeline sent a

smile past Lorne's shoulder in the moment before Lorne reached her.

Lorne wrapped her in his arms and pressed a light kiss to her forehead. "Good morning. You seemed to sleep well."

"I did." The best she'd slept in a long time. She guessed that likely had to do with the dragon she currently held. And perhaps she subconsciously felt more safe here in an inn within the borders of what was supposed to be an enemy kingdom than she did in her own bed at her own castle.

That instinct wasn't without cause. She was probably more at risk of assassination from her own people than she was from her enemy. Her lords had already tried to kill her. Twice.

Lorne took a step back and gestured toward a side table, where a large tray piled with dishes rested. "There's food, although it might have gone cold by now. We can request the kitchen send up more."

"I'll be fine." She made her way to the side table and investigated the remnants of food left on the tray. The toast, eggs, and sausages were looking rather cold and unappetizing, but she didn't want to delay everyone by asking for fresh food.

Lorne halted behind her, then grabbed the tray of food before she could take any of it. "There's no way you're eating that. I'll see about getting a fresh plate for you."

With that, he whisked the tray out of the room and disappeared, leaving her alone with Thaddeus and King Philip. Not a situation she'd ever envisioned.

"Come. Sit." King Philip gestured at the chair Lorne had vacated.

"We shouldn't linger too long." Adeline edged toward the chair, not sure if she dared face King Philip, now that she knew he was her father-in-law. Sure, he'd hugged her the night before. But that didn't erase the strange tension. "I'm not sure what kind of chaos is happening in Kelverny right now, and we really need to finish negotiating that peace treaty."

"Yes, but we have enough time for you to eat a hearty breakfast. No reason you need to go into the negotiations on an empty stomach." King Philip gave her a smile that was somehow parental, despite how awkward he too must feel. He cast a glance around the room and heaved a sigh. "As much as I'd love to suggest that we finish the treaty negotiations in comfort here, we can't risk the Kelvernese people believing I exerted undue influence over you or that you signed the peace treaty while under duress on Lalsacian soil."

"No." Adeline heaved a sigh of her own. It would have been much nicer to simply get the negotiations over with here in this comfortable room with its plush chairs rather than return to that tent between the battle lines. She stroked a hand over the fleech dragon's back. "I suppose I'll need to return this little one to the forest on our way."

"Actually, I think the dragon has bonded with you. I doubt he will leave, even if you give him the option." King Philip smiled, as if he was unconcerned that one of his kingdom's precious fleech dragons had bonded with the enemy queen.

"Sounds like someone else I know." She hadn't meant to trap this fleech dragon with her, any more than she'd meant to trap Lorne.

But had she trapped them? Or, as Lorne kept insisting, had they chosen her? Chosen to be with her, no matter what they were giving up to do so?

The thought of being chosen like that was so overwhelming that she couldn't quite fathom it. Her grandfather had certainly never chosen anyone with such a depth of love. Not her. Not his own son, whom he'd likely had a hand in killing. Even as king, he'd chosen his own power by inciting a war rather than doing what was truly good for his kingdom.

But there had been others. Hadn't Thaddeus and Jelsa shown her what chosen loyalty could look like? And all the guards who had remained loyal to her? They'd never swayed in their devotion, even when she was standing alone and vulnerable beneath her grandfather's dictates.

Could she choose them as wholeheartedly in return? Could she give her heart to her kingdom, her people, and to Lorne as completely as she ought?

CHAPTER SIXTEEN

The ride back to the battle lines gave them ample time to discuss the particulars of the treaty. By the time they reached the spot between the lines—the tent still set up for their use—it was a simple thing to write out what they'd discussed on the way there.

Sitting at a table set outside in full view of both armies, Adeline stared at the finished treaty, the quill to sign it in her hand. This was it. An end to the war. Peace. Everything her parents would have wanted. Everything she had risked her marriage, her life, and her reign to achieve.

She probably shouldn't be hesitating. Not that this was hesitation, exactly. More that this occasion felt too momentous to rush. She needed a few seconds to take it all in. Maybe then it would feel real.

Lorne's hand rested on her shoulder, the slight pressure of a squeeze grounding her in the moment.

She glanced over her shoulder at him where he

stood at her back. She appreciated that he was standing with her in this moment and not at his father's side on the other side of the table.

With a deep breath, she turned her focus back to the paper before her. She scrawled her signature on both copies of the treaty before she held out the pen to King Philip.

He took it and swiveled the copies of the treaty to face him. He didn't even pause before he signed each of them.

And just like that, the war was over. After all the blood that had been shed—after all her grandfather had done to prolong it including using her parents' deaths to start it—the war ended with a mere scratch of pen on page.

This wouldn't fix all of the tension within Kelverny. After all, she had not one, but two traitorous lords to sentence and very likely execute, and that wouldn't sit well with their supporters.

Nor would everyone in Kelverny be satisfied with the compromises in the treaty. Kelverny wouldn't gain any territory or any fleech dragons of their own. But Lalsacia had pledged to enable a way for Kelvernese citizens to cross the border and seek healing from the fleech dragons, under Lalsacian escort, of course. It would take a few months for Lalsacia to put infrastructure in place to make sure all the Kelvernese, Lalsacians, and fleech dragons involved remained safe. But it was a solution.

Kelverny, too, wouldn't be giving up any of the sylon cats. But they'd pledged military aid, including the use of their sylon cats, to Lalsacia in the event of an attack by another kingdom.

The stickiest situation to sort out had been the whole how-to-handle-the-heirs-being-married thing. As long as King Philip was alive, it was fairly manageable. He would rule Lalsacia while Adeline and Lorne made Kelverny their priority. Even after King Philip died, they could split their time between the kingdoms, assuming that the tensions had cooled to the point that neither kingdom worried too much if their monarch spent half the year in a different kingdom.

But it was the next generation where things got complicated. Their firstborn son couldn't inherit both kingdoms, not unless they wanted to merge the kingdoms into one. And while they certainly had hope that the two kingdoms would work their way toward a solid peace, they wouldn't be ready for that, even several decades down the road.

So instead, they'd worked out a whole bunch of succession contingencies, writing them into the treaty. They would have to tweak the succession laws in their respective kingdoms to match, but it was the best they could do.

At its heart, they'd agreed that the firstborn son would be the heir to Lalsacia while the firstborn daughter would be heir to Kelverny. There were a few contingencies, such as if they had only girls or only boys, but that was the simplest.

Kelverny's nobles might not appreciate the fact that their heir would be the daughter instead of the son. But as Adeline was the queen, it had made the most sense for Kelverny to be the one to have a daughter as heir. Hopefully by the time her daughter inherited the throne, Kelverny would be so used to having a queen that they would find it natural to have another one.

King Philip set down the pen, picked up one of the copies of the treaty, and pulled out his royal seal. A Lalsacian clerk hurried forward with a bowl of purple wax, already heated in preparation.

Thaddeus appeared at Adeline's elbow, a bowl of Kelvernese yellow wax heated and ready to go. She took her own royal ring off her finger to make pressing it into the wax easier.

After taking the bowl from Thaddeus, she poured a small amount of the wax onto the bottom of one of the treaties near her signature, then pressed her seal into it to make everything official. Once that was done, she passed that treaty to King Philip, who in turn passed her the treaty he'd already sealed. After repeating the process, she claimed one of the copies of the treaty for herself while King Philip took the other.

The two of them stood, and King Philip nodded to her. "I wish we had more time to get to know each other."

"Me too." Strangely, she found herself meaning that. "And I would have loved to spend more time in Lalsacia. The little I saw of it was lovely."

"Perhaps you will be able to visit again in a few months, once things settle." King Philip sent her a smile, but his gaze strayed to Lorne beside her.

She understood. It must be hard for the Lalsacian

king to send his only child back into a former enemy kingdom, not knowing when he'd see him again.

"I would like that." She smiled at the king before she turned to Lorne, resting a hand on his arm. "Take your time."

Then she headed for the gathering of Kelvernese nobles and soldiers farther up the valley, leaving Lorne to take a few moments to say farewell to his father.

Thaddeus joined her, walking just a few steps behind her. "You did it, Your Majesty."

"*We* did it." Adeline glanced at him, her smile seeming not enough to convey the depth of what was in her heart. "This was your plan. You were the one who suggested I marry the Lalsacian noble in the dungeon."

Thaddeus huffed, shook his head, and shot a look over his shoulder. "I might have considered the options more thoroughly if I'd known he was the Lalsacian crown prince and not just a high-ranking nobleman."

She would have too. But it was just as well. She couldn't imagine loving anyone else the way she did Lorne.

Facing her again, Thaddeus dipped his head in as respectful a bow as he could manage while they were walking. "But you were the one who risked everything to follow the plan I proposed. Do not sell yourself short, Your Majesty. This is your achievement."

Adeline straightened her shoulders, the thick paper of the treaty in her hand. Her grandfather never would have believed she was capable of this.

He'd dismissed her. Controlled her. Tried to break her.

But she had done it. Survived two assassination attempts. Brought about peace. Dare she hope this would earn the support of her nobility? Or, at least, enough support that they'd merely try to corral her with politics rather than take the leap to regicide. Political maneuvering, she could handle.

Just before she reached the line of Kelvernese nobles and soldiers, Lorne jogged to her side and clasped her hand. She peered up at him, searching the expression on his face. "Are you all right?"

"Yes." His smile remained unwavering, more than she would have expected.

She still studied his face, looking for what, she wasn't fully sure. Regret, maybe?

He swung their clasped hands, facing forward. "I mean it. Yes, I'll miss my father, and I'll miss Lalsacia. But this time, I'm bringing my horse along, and I gave a list of things I'd like sent to Kelverny to one of my father's clerks. This won't be like last time."

A quick glance over her shoulder showed that Godwin, Burchard, Arne, Emil, and Orvyn trailed after them, mounted on destriers and leading the black warhorse she and Lorne had ridden on that mad dash to Lalsacia.

The sight made her smile once again. Their loyalty wasn't something to take for granted. After all they'd endured in Kelverny, they were still willing to return to continue guarding Lorne.

Although, she suspected Orvyn's return had as

much to do with the fact that Jelsa was in Kelverny as it was loyalty to his prince.

"No, it won't." She would make sure of it.

More, she was going to stop cutting him out. The nobles might complain, but she needed Lorne at her side in his full capacity as her prince consort. And when she had the chance to visit Lalsacia, she would embrace her role at his side as his princess.

It was time to finally be bold and speak the truth of her heart. She halted and turned to better face him. "I love you. I know you might not believe that after I tried to send you back to Lalsacia, but—"

He pulled her into his arms and kissed her, right there in the valley in the sight of the armies of both their kingdoms.

And she didn't even care. She was kissing him and he was kissing her and they loved each other. That was all that mattered.

With a flap and rustle of wings, the little yellow-green fleech dragon barreled through the air and slammed into her. Breaking off the kiss, she fumbled to wrap an arm around him as he clung to the front of her dress with his claws. "I guess you're coming home with me."

Lorne's grin widened. "Yes. Let's go home."

Adeline cradled their newborn daughter, taking in her tiny face, tiny nose, tiny fingers. "She's perfect."

Lorne wrapped one arm around her shoulders as he stretched out on the bed beside her. In his other arm, he held their newborn son. "And so is our son."

"Twins." Adeline shook her head before she rested it against his shoulder. "The midwife guessed as much, but I still can hardly believe it. An heir for both Kelverny and Lalsacia. Both kingdoms will be pleased."

After some initial argument over being assigned a female heir in the treaty, the nobles had, eventually, come to terms with it. As she'd earned their overall support, if not their loyalty, the Kelvernese nobles—and most importantly the common people—had embraced having a queen. They'd embrace their new princess just as much, and probably feel a sense of pride that they were the ones who would have Adeline's and Lorne's firstborn child for their heir.

Kelverny's new crown princess had beaten her brother to being the firstborn by a mere three minutes.

"Forget the kingdoms for a moment." Lorne pressed a kiss to her temple. "Today is for us and our family."

"Yes." Adeline snuggled closer to Lorne, even as their daughter slept peacefully in her arms.

They'd come to Lalsacia for the baby's birth—better to have more than one fleech dragon on hand—and they were currently residing in one of the royal family's country estates, away from the prying eyes of both kingdoms.

Chitter, the fleech dragon who had bonded to her, currently slept at the end of the bed. The little dragon had been a faithful companion in the past two years, calming her during intense meetings with the council and during public appearances. The dragon's presence had done much in helping her heal from her grandfather's years of control and manipulation.

Although, Lorne certainly had played a large part as well.

There came a knock on the door before it cracked open. "May we come in?"

Lorne shared a look with her, and she gave him a nod. He raised his voice. "Yes, of course."

King Philip stepped inside, his gaze sweeping over them as he smiled. He sat in the chair beside the bed, his eyes wide with wonder.

Thaddeus trailed after him, halting in the doorway as if he didn't dare fully step into the room. But he'd been more a father to her than anyone else in the past few years, and it had seemed only right to invite him to visit as family in the wake of their children's births. After all, he was the reason she and Lorne had married.

"Meet your granddaughter, Princess Soraine of Kelverny." Lorne's voice held such pride that Adeline's chest filled with it.

"And your grandson, Prince Sorran of Lalsacia." Adeline sat up straighter as she nodded to the babe Lorne held. "Would you like to hold them? Or, well, one of them?"

King Philip mutely nodded, and Lorne eased the newborn Sorran into his arms. Cradling his grandson, King Philip looked at the baby with such love that something in Adeline's chest both ached and healed all at once.

Her children wouldn't have a grandfather like she had. They would be well loved, not just by their parents, but also by their grandfather. Given the adoring look Thaddeus was sending the babies, they'd be loved by their adopted grandfather as well. They wouldn't be valued only because they were in line for the thrones but loved because of who they were.

"And you too, Thaddeus." Lorne gestured the steward closer. "Come hold your new princess."

Once Thaddeus had perched in the other chair, Adeline passed Soraine to him. It seemed right that Thaddeus should be one of the first to hold her.

When Lorne wrapped his arm around her once again, Adeline leaned into him, even as he pressed a light kiss to her temple.

She had a husband who loved her. Twins to pour

their shared love into. A kingdom to rule in a far better manner than it had been before.

It was more than Adeline could have imagined on that desperate night when she'd taken the chance to marry the Lalsacian in the dungeon. But she wouldn't have it any other way.

ACKNOWLEDGMENTS

Thanks so much for reading *Hearts and Shadows*! I hope this story was as healing and cozy for you as it was for me. As many of you know, I wrote this book after losing my dog in November of 2025. It was the low stress, short book I needed during a difficult time in my life, and it is my hope that it provides the same escape for you.

If you ever find typos in my books, feel free to message me on social media or send me an email through the Contact Me page of my website.

If you want to learn about all my upcoming releases, sign up for my newsletter, and get a full list of my books, head over to www.taragrayce.com.

Did you know that if you sign up for my newsletter, you'll receive lots of free goodies? You will receive the free novella *Steal a Swordmaiden's Heart*, which is set in the same world as *Stolen Midsummer Bride* and *Bluebeard and the Outlaw*! This novella is a prequel to *Stolen Midsummer Bride,* and tells the story of how King

Theseus of the Court of Knowledge won the hand of Hippolyta, Queen of the Swordmaidens.

If you don't wish to sign up for my newsletter, *Steal a Swordmaiden's Heart* is available on Amazon, though it isn't in KU like the rest of the series.

You will also receive the free novella *Torn Curtains*, a fantasy Regency Beauty and the Beast retelling. This one isn't available anywhere else besides my newsletter!

Sign up for my newsletter now

As always, thank you to my friends and family for all they do to love and support me both with my writing and with life. Seriously, I'm so grateful for each and everyone one of you!

Thank you to Bethany and Deborah for proofing the book and making sure it read as smoothly as possible. Thank you to everyone from the cover designer (Get Covers) to Liz Brand (audiobook narrator) for bringing this book to life!

Thank you most of all to Jesus, my Savior, who brought me through a difficult winter.